Hood to Hood: A Cleveland Story

D. M. Gaines

New Flavor
Books

W

Hood to Hood: A Cleveland Story

ISBN:978-0692371220 (New Flavor Books & Publishing, LLC)

Congress Control Number: 2013937259

Copy/editing and cover design by
Earvin Taze Watters Jr.
ezatcreations@yahoo.com
Revised *January 2015*

www.newflavorbooksandpublishingllc.com
New Flavor Books is an imprint of New Flavor Books & Publishing LLC

New Flavor Books & Publishing LLC
P.O. Box 603323 Cleveland, Ohio 44103

Dedication

This book is dedicated to anyone that has found themselves trapped inside a hood in any part of the US, hopefully one day you will find a way out

Acknowledgement

I would like to give thanks to the following people: Batman and Donnie Ru from California, thanks for your input, to Poetic Gangster for encouraging me to write to BK and CJ for reading my books and giving me feedback, y'all kept it real. Lastly, to all of you that bought the first version of the book, even though it wasn't totally together you still gave me a chance, I appreciate that. – Donny G

Prologue

When people talk of the cities with a high poverty and crime rate, they are quick to mention Detroit, New York, Chicago and St. Louis. Cleveland, Ohio is often left out. Cleveland is in the top ten of the biggest cities in America and it is full of crime and poverty. The suburbs of Cleveland also slowly turned into slums. Do to the revitalization of the inner city, the lower class people were pushed out to the suburbs through a housing assistance program called Section 8. Cleveland has led the nation with the highest murder rate a couple of times. Even Bloods and Crips rose up in a large part of the city. Violence became an everyday occurrence. For those of you who do not know, the hoods are similar all around the world. They contain the same elements. Let me take you on a trip through mines.

"Yo Derrick!"

"What's up dawg?" Tee yelled.

"Ain't shit Tee just about to go to the store to get a forty."

Derrick was a short, dark skinned cat who lived up the hill in Rainbow Terrace, which is a housing complex across from Garden Valley. He is a part-time hustler. He grew up with two parents in his household and graduated from high school, but lost ambition to do anything else. He refused to attend college, even after being offered a scholarship. Derrick told his parents he could not find a job, although he never did any real job hunting. His father tried to encourage him to join the military service. His response was, "I'm not joining no white man's army." He decided to take to the streets as a petty hustler. He didn't see anything beyond waking up every day and chilling in the projects.

Tee resided down the hill in Garden Valley. He was a six foot tall dude with broad shoulders, who loved to fight. Usually he would be the one to start them. He had been in and out of jail his whole life. He was raised by a single mother, with four brothers and sisters, they never had much. Tee used to get teased as a kid for wearing second hand clothes. He had many fights, which helped hone his skills.

By the time he turned thirteen, he grew to be almost six feet tall and started to bully the bullies. Tee also changed his living conditions by engaging in all kinds of criminal activity. He robbed, committed burglaries and even used extortion.

One day he drove up the hill in search of Ron. Ron had borrowed $300.00 from Tee in a crap game. He asked Derrick, "Have you seen that nigga Ron?"

"No why?"

"The nigga owe me some money and keep ducking me."

"You know everybody supposed to go up to the courts to play ball at three, Ron ass ain't missing no game." Derrick told him.

"Yeah I'm going to shoot up there myself, that nigga go make me bust his shit!"

"When you get ready to roll through, come and swoop me." stated Derrick.

"Alright, I got you."

Tee jumped in his car and road out, pissed because he had been looking for Ron for the past three days. Ron was down to his last $40.00. If he don't find Ron soon, he is going to be forced to hit a lick.

Derrick went to the store and copped a forty ounce, then headed over to Stacey's house. Stacey was his little jump off, a 23-year old chick that had her own apartment that she shared with her 2-year old son, Junior. Stacey worked at Cleveland Clinic as a nurse's aide. She made enough money for her and her baby to live comfortably.

Her and Derrick met one day at Dave's Eagles grocery store. Derrick was outside chilling with a couple fellas when she came out carrying two bags and offered his help. Stacey reluctantly accepted. By the time they reached her apartment Derrick had found out she had recently moved there and did not have a man, that's all he needed to know. By day's end, Stacey belonged to him. It has been over a year now.

He got to Stacey's house and pulled out the extra key that she gave him. He stepped in to see Stacey sitting on the couch watching TV.

"Boy what took you so long?"

"I stopped to talk to Tee."

"You need to stay away from Tee, he ain't nothing but trouble."

"That's my nigga, he alright."

"Okay, he alright, if you end up locked up fucking with him, he better be the one to pay your bond!"

"Girl you tripping, do you want to smoke this blunt or what?"

"Fire it up just don't forget what I said."

Stacey liked Derrick because he treated her and her son like his own family. She originally came from Cleveland Heights. She grew up with a healthy family upbringing. Her mother had goals for her, and she had dreams of one day becoming a physician. Stacey is smart, at least when it came to textbooks, men were a different story. During her second year in college, she started messing with a street hustler that got her pregnant. By the time Stacey had her baby, the dude got locked up. After giving birth she had to drop out of school. Her dream downsized from being a doctor, to being a nurse's aide. She signed up for public housing, and a year later was given an apartment in the Rainbow Terrace projects. She hoped one day Derrick would get it together, and find a job, so she could go back and finish school. She even had thoughts of them possibly getting married.

Tee was driving with his music turned up bumping Scarface, when his cellphone rang. He turned the music down, grabbed his phone and saw that it was Kayla calling. He decided to answer it.

"What's up ma?"

"Nothing, just sitting here bored, I wanted to see what you were doing, and if you wanted to come by."

I got to go up to the courts at three, but I got a couple hours to spare.

"Is it going be worth my time?"

"Don't I always make it worth your time?"

"Don't I give it to you every way you like it?"

"Girl, you ain't never lied, my dick is getting hard just thinking about you. Look I'm going to stop and grab something to smoke, and then I'm on my way bet?"

"Alright nigga, I will be waiting on your ass, so hurry up while this pussy is wet as fuck."

"Say no more, I'm out." Tee responded as he closed his phone and turned his music back up. He headed up to 79th and Woodland to purchase a bag of purple haze. He figured he could smoke with Kayla, get some good head and chill for a couple hours, before going up to the courts to catch Ron.

Ron chilled up in Rainbow Terrace over Dre's house. Ron grew up in the King Kennedy Projects. He got caught up in so much trouble that he was forced to relocate. He's always been a fuck up pulling scams and trying to swindle people any way he could. He was raised by his grandmother and as a young boy he used to hold drugs for the old heads up on the pill block. Back then his age helped him stay alive. But after a while the old heads figured out that he stole out the packs.

That day he was playing Madden, at Dre's house with Bobby and Mike. Dre had only been staying in Rainbow Terrace for six months. He was originally from East Cleveland, which used to be a suburb of Cleveland originally having its own police department and Mayor. Now it had deteriorated to a suburban slum. Dre was cool, and everybody in Rainbow Terrace liked him. He was tall, slim and dark skinned. He wore waves in his hair and had a chipped tooth. People liked him because he was silly and loved cracking jokes. Since he stayed by his self, most of the fellas would swing by to play the PlayStation, shoot dice or just smoke, drink and chill.

Ron and Bobby were going head to head when Mike stated, "Y'all know everybody go be at the courts at three."

"Word!" replied Ron.

"Yeah, Longwood supposed to play against the Valley. Niggas bringing cases, smoke and you know all the bitches go be up there sack chasing."

"Say no more, your boy Ron is there."

"What time is it now?" Ron asked.

"One thirty" replied Mike.

"We got another hour for me to beat y'all asses," Bobby stated.

"Aye, where that nigga Dre at?" Mike asked.

"That nigga in his room fucking that stripper bitch, Rhonda" responded Ron.

"Stacey's sister Rhonda?"

"Yeah that's the one."

"Man, that bitch live, why he got that bitch locked in there by himself?" Mike asked.

"Shit, I don't know, go ask him."

"Say no more, I'm about to get my dick sucked." said Mike.

Mike headed down the hall to Dre's bedroom. He approached the door and put his ear to it and listened. He heard noises and the bed squeaking. He tapped on the door, and Dre answered.

"What's up?"

"Aye, this Mike open the door nigga I got to holla at you about something."

"Man I'm busy, call me later."

"Man, I know you in there with Rhonda."

"I'm trying to holla at her right quick."

"You tripping holla at her later."

"Yeah, whatever captain save a hoe." Mike responded as he headed back down the hallway.

"What happened?" asked Ron, when he saw Mike enter the living room.

"Man that fag ass nigga cock blocking."

"Well it's going to be mad bitches at the courts."

"You got to put your game down."

"You best believe it!" responded Mike.

"What that nigga want with you?" Dre asked Rhonda.

"Hell if I know, maybe he is trying to spend some money."

"Well he got to see you on his own time. Now turn around and get on your knees." Dre told her as he eased up to hit her from behind.

Tee arrived at Kayla's house. She let him in, wearing only a short t-shirt that left her ass and pussy fully exposed. Tee reached out and picked her up by the ass cheeks. She wrapped her legs around his waist. He used the back of his foot to kick the door shut. He walked with her towards the couch. He dropped her on it. Kayla went straight for his belt buckle. Tee reached into his pocket and pulled out a blunt and fired it up. Kayla had his dick out and was sucking on it. Tee took a deep inhale from the blunt, and then slowly started blowing the smoke out, creating a cloud above Kayla's head. Tee looked down at Kayla. The weed had a hypnotic effect on him. He just stared down at her sucking him off and enjoyed the feeling. He put one foot up on the couch, and put one hand on the back of her head. As he guided her head up and down his dick, he said to her, "That's it baby girl suck that dick, just like that." Kayla made muffled sounds as she picked up the pace. Saliva drooled out the side of her mouth all over Tee's dick. Tee was floating. The combination of the weed and the head had him in ecstasy. He started losing control. He put his other hand on her head and held it still as he started fucking her mouth. Kayla was gagging and choking, but that didn't slow Tee down. He continued to ram rod her mouth. All of a sudden his body started shaking and he rose up on his toes and started blasting his cum in Kayla's mouth. Kayla was choking and could not breathe. She took her hands and pushed him off of her and fell to the floor gasping for air. Tee stood over her still cumming, using his hand to milk the rest out onto her face and chest.

Once Kayla caught her breath she slapped Tee on his leg and said, "You crazy motherfucker you could have killed me!" Tee just looked down at her with a demonic look in his eyes and smiled. Kayla thought to herself, this nigga really is crazy. She got up off the floor and went to the bathroom to clean herself up. Tee fixed his pants, sat down and lit up another blunt. After Kayla fixed herself, she returned to the living room and sat down next to Tee. She laughed, and punched him in the arm and said, "Nigga you crazy for real." Tee did not respond instead he passed her the blunt, which she eagerly accepted. She took a deep pull and immediately started coughing. Once her coughing subsided she said, "Damn that shit is strong."

"Only the best for the best."

"Does that include me too?"

"Fo sho, but look I got to bounce, I got a nigga to see."

"Damn, you picking a nigga over me?"

"Nope, this about money baby girl, I'm tired of this nigga ducking me."

"So when am I go see you again?"

"Shit! A bitch needs to get hers too."

"Look I'm gone try to get back with you tonight, maybe spend the night and tax that ass."

"Don't play with me Tee. You always be selling me dreams."

"Don't worry about it, I got you." He jumped in his car, started it, cranked his music and headed for the courts.

Down in Longwood a group of guys were congregating in a parking lot, talking about the upcoming game. There were ten guys that were going to play, and another fifteen that were going to support them. The leader of the pack, whose name was Spank, started addressing the group.

"Look y'all we going up here to show them busters how we do it. We ain't taking any shorts. They got us last year, but this our year."

Spank stood 6' 3". He was slim and very athletic. He was a star basketball player for East Tech high school until he dropped out in the eleventh grade to pursue his dreams of getting rich. However, the way in which he originally wanted to pursue those dreams changed from playing basketball to selling drugs. Spank was a natural leader, and he took his leadership skills from the basketball court to the drug trade. He assembled a group of guys to help him push drugs through Longwood, as well as other parts of Cleveland. His right hand man was Tink. It's ironic that they called him Tink being that he stood at 6' 2", weighed a solid two fifty and packed one hell of a knockout punch. Tink was more like an enforcer for the crew, handling any problems that may arise concerning collecting money and turf disputes. He was respected and only has a soft spot for one person, his girl Coco.

"Man fuck those niggas." stated Sean. Sean was second in command. He distributed all the dope to the lower level guys and counted the money. He was a short cat, kind of pudgy. He finished school and went to college majoring in Business Management. He was good with numbers. He was also a good communicator with people skills, which made him an asset. But he wasn't raised in the projects and did not have to sell drugs. It was the excitement that attracted him. Lastly, there was Allen who would oversee all the little runners on the block. How a pimp watched over his hoes is how Allen watched over the workers. He was there for protection and to make sure that they were putting in work and not bullshitting. Allen had a rep for busting his guns and not taking any bullshit. He was born and raised in the Longwood housing projects, and represented them to the fullest.

Those four rode hard together and had Longwood on lock. Spank had advertised the upcoming game that he was sponsoring and held tryouts. He picked nine people to play alongside himself and those that didn't make it will still go to show support. The parking lot was crowded. There were several groups of girls that were there as well. This was to be a big event that had been taking place for the last two years. It drew a large crowd, and lots of money was bet on the game. Plus, whichever project won, got bragging rights. Tink's girl Coco stood outside of her Lexus truck talking to her friends.

"Girl I hope these niggas don't get up there and start tripping."

"You know them niggas go end up fighting, they always do." responded her friend Silvia.

"Girl, I just hope they don't get to shooting." chimed her other girl Linda.

"Shit! Look at all these niggas. There's bound to be some bullshit." replied Coco.

"Fuck it! We can just sit in the car and watch. If shit starts popping off we can just roll out." Silvia stated.

"It ain't that simple, you know Tink got me riding with the guns."

"Girl you dumb as fuck, you go end up going to jail for him." Linda said.

"Bitch who you think bought me this truck?"

"My nigga down for me and I'm down for him. I'm a ride or die chick and I'm riding for mine. So if you got a problem with me having guns in the car then find you another source of transportation!"

"Damn you be catching an attitude. I'm go ride, but if shit starts popping off I'm go hop my ass on the bus to get back home." stated Linda.

Coco and Tink had been messing around since they were in high school. Before Tink had any type of money she was with him. Once he got on, he stayed the same. He didn't start tripping on her, and kept it real, and for that she will always be by his side.

Sean was sitting in his Beamer when his phone rang. He answered it, "Who dis?"

"Man, its Rick from the black"

"What's up Rick?"

"I need a whole thang."

"Nigga, when you start copping that much work?"

"Man skip all that, you trying to get this paper or what?"

Sean thought for a second and realized that $26,000 was a lot to pass up. Rick usually wasn't good for more than a half, but maybe he had been stacking his money or was going in with somebody else. Whatever the case may be he told his self he had to get that money.

He was thinking, he can bust that move and get to the Valley by the time the game gets good.

"Hey Rick, give me about a half an hour and I will be there."

"All right, my nigga. I'll be in the back parking lot."

"Alright one." replied Sean. He walked over to Spank, who was in his car about to pull off.

"Spank!"

"Hold up!" he yelled out. Spank threw the car back in park.

"What's up?"

"I'm going catch up, after I make this run. That nigga Rick out of Morris Black is trying to cop a whole one."

"When that bum ass nigga start copping whole bricks?"

"The boy been on the come up lately."

"You got your strap?"

"Yeah, you know I keep that."

"Good, just in case you got to lay his faggot ass down. Handle that, and then meet us up at the courts."

"Bet." said Sean as he started back towards his car.

Spank pulled off as the lead car, with the rest of the convoy following him. It was all makes, and models from Regals, Lexus' to Escalades. All riding back to back, headed towards the valley.

Fred, Doc and Ronald were standing in front of a Jamaican restaurant called Dailey's. All three were from the 116th and Buckeye area. They all grew up together. They attended the same schools and even played on the same pee wee football team together. Fred was the unofficial leader of the three, mostly because he was the more outspoken and aggressive one. He stood about 5' 9" and weighed two hundred and fifteen pounds. He had done a couple prison bits. He was locked up for everything from hitting jewelry licks to selling dope. He had been out of prison for eight months now, and had been trying to come back up through the dope game. Fred was the type that tried to get the most out of everything. He didn't even have to chance being out on the hot blocks. He bought enough dope to sell weight, yet he chose to break his dope down and sell it piece by piece. Sometime he would cook up a quarter Key, cut it down and sell all in stones, tripling his profit. Doc and Ronald would sometimes ride him for being so greedy but Fred would just laugh and say, "I got to get all mines."

Everybody liked him because, he was silly, and had an easy going personality. Doc spoke up, "Man it's slow as hell out here."

"Yeah this shit crazy!" said Ronald.

Doc was a year younger than Fred. At 31 years old. He was a pretty boy type, slim, high yellow with 360 waves. He thought he was a certified hoe knocker and he did bag more women than anybody else in his crew. But that gave him four different baby mommas. He put more effort into dressing fly than he did into taking care of his kids. At 31 years old he still lived in his mother's basement.

"Let's go up to RD's." said Ronald, who rounded out the click. He was the smallest, being only 5' 5" and weighing a hundred and fifty pounds. Ronald was a tennis shoe hustler. Out of the ten years that he had been hustling he has never bought more than two ounces at one time. He usually never had more than re up money. All his profits went into buying clothes and raggedy cars. Even though Fred was in prison for three years he was still serving Ronald packages.

Fred spoke up, "Y'all know that hoe Shannon who I be messing with from the Valley? She told me that Longwood is supposed to be coming up there to play the Valley in basketball today."

"So what, y'all want to roll down there?" asked Ronald.

"It's up to y'all. We can ride down there in my shit."

"It's all good, you know them niggas be on some bullshit sometimes." stated Doc.

"Nigga!"

"We going strapped anyway. They get on some bullshit, and then we get on so bullshit!" replied Fred.

"Fuck them niggas, let's roll!" stated Ronald.

"Alright, but let me see if my jerk chicken is ready, then we can roll out." said Fred.

"Damn this pussy wet!" Derrick said out loud as he fucked Stacey. They had smoked two blunts earlier and drank a forty ounce. Stacey started feeling freaky. She reached over and started rubbing his dick. Once his dick got hard that's all it took. He stripped her right there on the couch. Stacey had her legs spread and bent back to her chest, with her hands behind her knees holding them in that position as he fucked her. She was sweating and making fuck faces as he stroked her. Derrick had his arms on the armrest for support, and was watching his dick go in and out of her. He started picking up his rhythm and felt that he was only seconds away from cumming. Stacey knew that he was on the verge, so she picked up her pace as she gyrated her hips. She also used her hands to grip his back and pulled him closer to her. She wanted to feel him all the way up in her. Derrick took his arms off of the armrest and let his self sink all the way into her. He came out until only the head was in, and then slammed back into her. Stacey told him, "That's it, come on baby let it go."

He tensed up, "I'm about to cum, I'm about to cum."

"Me too!" They both trembled and convulsed. After they stopped, Derrick rolled of her and looked at the clock.

He said, "Shit it's two thirty!"

"I got to get ready for the game. I'm going to page Tee and jump in the shower. If he calls back before I get out tell him I said come get me."

"Yeah alright nigga, but I told your ass that he's in trouble, and if you find yourself in trouble with him, you are going to be stuck."

"Yeah, whatever girl, you ain't go let this dick stay away from you too long."

"Okay Mr. Good dick we will see."

Stacey heard all the rumors about Tee, and felt like everybody can't be lying on him. For some reason she can't get Derrick to see that and it frustrated her.

☐

Rick was up in Morris Black projects. He was in the back parking lot, talking with two other guys. They were planning the robbery of Sean once he arrived with the key of dope. The two guys with him were Tony and Man, who were cousins. They were both 22 years old. Tony was tall at 6' 2" and Man was short at 5' 6", but they were both equally violent. People thought that Man had a short man's complex because of how violently he reacted in situations that did not necessarily call for violence. Man was quick to bust his guns also, which kept people very leery of him. Tony used to be alright until he started smoking wet.

One of his old flames slipped him a wet stick. He became addicted, and hasn't been the same ever since. Once he started smoking heavy, he began thinking why sell dope, when I can just rob the dope boys. He brought the idea to Man, who never was a real hustler and was always a follower. Man readily agreed to the idea. They've been robbing dope boys all over the city for the past two years. They have both been shot at as well as shot, leaving Tone having to wear a shit bag for six months. But they've never truly hit a big lick, because they mostly rob dudes on the block that are not going to carry a large amount drugs or cash on them. They were glad that Rick pulled them in on the lick.

"Look he is going to meet me back here." Rick explained.

"Ain't shit to worry about, I cop from him all the time so he ain't going to suspect nothing."

"Peep Man, you go be with me. I'm go act like we going half."

"Tone you wait in the hallway until he pulls up, once we get in the car with him, you come out and act like you walking past. When I give the signal, you do your thing."

"You want me strapped too?" asked Man.

"Yeah, you go get in the backseat, and when he pulls out the brick you go up pipe. Once he up pipe, then you run up on the car to back him up Tone." Rick told them.

"Rick you know that's going to look like a straight set up." Tone stated.

"Nigga I don't give a fuck what it looks like!"

"I'm trying to come up!"

"Shit, he don't know us anyway, so if you don't give a fuck then we sure don't give a fuck." replied Man.

Rick developed a grudge for everyone who was at the place he thought he should be in life. Back in the early 90's there were a lot of Jamaicans in Cleveland. The Jamaicans would plug into people that were already in the game and either front them dope or give them good prices. One Jamaican named Paul had taken a liking to Rick and started fronting him dope. In no time, Rick elevated in the game. With an endless supply of good dope, he quickly rose up in the ranks. Along with his rise, came his buying of many material assets. His only flaw was that he did not believe in saving money. His motto was, "It's mines, I spend it." He did not save money, so he would not be prepared if the inevitable was to ever happen. He caught a case when he served an informant that was wearing a wire a key of coke.

He sold his cars to pay for a lawyer and still received three years. While he was doing his bid, Paul was robbed and murdered. Once Rick was released he was almost broke, back at square one. He only had his jewelry left, which he had to sell to get a package. Without the backing he once had with Jamaican Paul he found it hard to elevate back to the status he once had. He was now seeing certain people in the game at the point where he felt he should be. It infuriated him, so he figured if he robs a couple big timers he could get back to the status he once had.

Sean was about to be his first lick. Even though Sean rides with a click, he felt that he is soft and is not from his hood, so there wouldn't be much to worry about. He knew Tone and Man from back in the day. He knew how they got down so he approached them about the caper, promising them a quarter bird a piece, they readily agreed.

Now they were just waiting for their vic to come. Sean had just left his house from picking up the package, when his phone rang, "What up?" he spoke into the phone.

"Hey Sean this Nena,"

"Damn where you been girl!"

"I was out of town for a while."

"You know I been missing that pussy right?"

"That's why I called you to see if you wanted to kick it."

"Shit! I'm about to make a run, then I got to go down to the Valley. We are playing a ball game against the Valley niggas. You can roll if you want to."

"That's cool can you pick me up from my friend Tammy's house?"

"She stays on Sophia right?"

"Yeah, the second house from the corner."

"That's right down the street from where I'm going. I'll swoop by and pick you up."

"Okay, I will be waiting." she replied.

Sean knew that he shouldn't mix business with pleasure, but the thought of fucking Nena clouded his judgment. She had some of the best pussy that he ever had. Not only that, she gave crazy head. Sean felt that if he did not snatch her up now, she may make other plans later on. He did not want to chance that. So he headed to pick her up.

Nena was a fly girl. Originally from New York, having moved to Cleveland in her late teens, she did everything from stripping to doing hair. Sean met her at Monroe's strip club, on the west side. She traveled doing feature shows at strip clubs all around the country. Sean and Nena have been fucking off and on for over a year now ever since, with no strings attached. Whenever she's in town, Sean is her first choice for a booty call.

.

6

The caravan of cars from Longwood was heading for the valley. There was a bridge to cross to reach the Valley when coming from their direction. Unknown to them, the police were set up on the other side of the bridge doing a traffic stop. They had radars trying to catch people speeding. The convoy was actually moving within the speed limit. Coco was last in the convoy and got caught at the red light that was posted before you go across the bridge. So in an effort to catch back up with the convoy, when the light turned green Coco sped up. When she came across the bridge a motorcycle cop with a radar gun pointed her way. The officer clocked her doing 45mph in a 35mph zone. He pulled out behind her with his lights flashing.

"Shit!"

"The police!" Coco said out loud.

"Girl you got them guns in here, I can't go to jail!" said Linda.

"Bitch shut the fuck up and chill I got this!" Coco told her as she pulled over.

"I'm telling you Coco you better take them out!"

"If they find them, I'm not going to jail for you or that nigga!"

"Don't make me fuck you up!"

"Now shut up, here he comes!"

The cop approached the driver's side, and tapped on the window. Coco rolled the window down and said, "Yes officer," in her sexiest voice.

"License and registration please,"

Coco reached in her purse and retrieved them, and handed them to the officer. The officer was looking everyone in the car over.

"Where you girls are off to in such a hurry? You were doing ten miles over the speed limit."

Linda started to say something, when Coco cut her off, "Officer I got a call saying that my mother had to be rushed to the hospital because of a possible heart attack, I am just anxious to get there to make sure that she is alright."

The officer asked, "What hospital was she taken to?"

"Saint Luke's!" replied Coco.

"Look," the officer said, handing back her license and registration, "I can understand that, I'll let you go with a warning, but I might not be so understanding next time."

"Yes officer, thank you very much."

The officer returned to his motorcycle, started it and pulled off. Once the officer pulled off, Coco turned to Linda and said, "Bitch! Get out!"

"What? You tripping." said Linda.

"Fuck that! Get your scary ass out my car! You might tell something!" Coco shouted.

"Fuck it! I'll get out but you got me fucked up." Linda opened the car door and got out.

"Naw bitch! You got yourself fucked up!" Coco replied as she turned and told Silvia to get in the front seat. Silvia climbed out of the back and got in the front. Coco pulled off mad as hell.

Silvia broke out laughing, "Damn girl you ain't have to do her like that."

"You want to be next?" That took the smile off of Silvia's face and they rode the rest of the way in silence.

Dre and Rhonda came out of the bedroom and entered the living room.

"Here go that captain save a hoe ass nigga right here." Mike said.

"Who your punk ass calling captain save a hoe?" asked Dre.

"And who you calling a hoe?" asked Rhonda.

"I'm talking to both you mother fuckers, what y'all bitches got beef?" Mike asked.

"Mike, get up out of my spot before I fuck you up!" Dre said in a raised tone.

"Nigga what's up then," Mike said as he approached Dre with his fist raised. Dre seen that he was serious and threw his hands up.

"Man y'all niggas chill!" Ron said, as he got up from the couch.

"Fuck that! This nigga thinks I'm sweet!" responded Dre, as he took a swing at Mike. Dre had heart but he really wasn't a good fighter. He swung wildly. Mike ducked then lashed out with a three piece combination, all of which connected and sent Dre to his ass. Ron rushed over and grabbed Mike to prevent him from doing more harm to Dre.

"Let me go and see what this bitch talking about now." Mike said.

"Man, you can't jump on her." Ron told him.

"Mike, I don't see what you mad at me for. You know I'm bout my money. He paid me so I was on his time." Rhonda stated.

"I can't believe you tripping bout some pussy that ain't even yours." Ron told him.

"I ain't tripping about no pussy, it's the principalities, and niggas got to respect my gangsta."

Dre who was still dazed got up off the couch and said, "Man I ain't with this, y'all clear out."

Ron called to everybody, "Come on y'all let's head down to the courts." Ron, Bobby and Mike headed out the door. Rhonda stayed to make sure that Dre was good.

Tee felt his two way start to vibrate. He took it off his hip looked at the number and couldn't place it. He picked up his cell and dialed the number. A female answered, "Hello?"

"Yo, who dis?" Tee asked.

"Nigga don't be calling here, talking about no who dis, who you trying to speak to?" asked Stacey.

"Whoa lil momma, I'm just returning a page. Someone paged me from this number and I didn't know who it was."

"My bad, this must be Tee?"

"Yeah this Tee, so now who is this?"

"This Stacey, Derrick paged you. He in the shower and wanted to make sure you pick him up on your way to the courts."

"Stacey what's up girl? You still mean as hell? I'm glad he did page me I forgot, tell him I'm on my way, alright?"

"Yeah I will tell him," Stacey said and then hung up.

7

Sean pulled up in front of Tammy's house and blew the horn. Seconds later Nena came out looking like a dime. Sean was glad that he stopped to pick her up. Nena was 5' 6" with a small waist and a pretty face. She had an ass shaped like a beach ball that jiggled loosely when she walked. When she got in the car she said, "Hey daddy."

When she closed the door, her scent filled the car. Sean loved the way she stayed smelling good, as well as how good she tasted.

"Daddy missed you." he told her as he smiled.

Sean turned his music up and drove off.

Rick and Man were sitting inside of Rick's Regal smoking a blunt.

"Man that nigga know I don't be copping this amount of work, that's why I didn't ask him to bring more. I know he scared about bringing me a whole one." Rick told Man.

"Fuck it! It will all add up dawg, we just take whatever we can get."

Rick sat up when he saw a car approaching.

"That's him right there."

"Shit, it looks like he got somebody in the passenger seat." Man stated.

"Fuck! This nigga had to put a monkey wrench in the game." Rick said angrily.

"So what's up now?"

"We follow through, we lay him and whoever he got with him down."

"Call Tone's cell and tell him to get ready."

Sean didn't like Morris Black because it did not have any streets that ran through it. If you pulled all the way in and something jumped off you would be shit out of luck. Sean had known Rick since before he did his bit, and when he was on top of his game. That's why he did not too much worry about going up in Morris Black. As he drove towards the back parking lot he reached under the seat and grabbed his pistol and placed it between the door and the seat. He felt that he might be alright with Rick, but it was still a lot of grimy niggas up there. The Black as it's called is referred to as being one of the roughest projects in Cleveland.

Sean saw Rick's Regal in the last parking space and pulled in beside it. He looked over and was surprised to see someone else sitting in the car with Rick. Rick gave a phony smile and exited his car carrying a Gucci pouch. Rick approached Sean's car. Sean rolled the window down and said, "What's up with that dude?"

"He straight, that's my nigga, he going in half with me on the package."

"I respect that, but I'm only doing business with you."

"Don't trip dawg it ain't like you came by yourself."

"Do you have the money?"

"It's right here!" Rick pointed to the pouch.

"Alright you get in, dude can wait where he at."

"No problem." Rick said as he reached for the back door handle.

Things weren't going as planned for Rick. He did not have a pistol on him, so he hoped that Tone and Man would improvise. He nervously got in the back seat.

Sean was grabbing the brick out of his secret compartment when he saw a figure in his side view mirror. A tall, slim, dude with a hat pulled low over his eyes was walking towards his car. At that moment a car door closed on the other side of the car. He turned the other way and saw the guy who was sitting in Rick's car previously now standing outside of it with both of his hands in his jacket pockets. Sean reached down and gripped his pistol.

"Man, I hope you ain't on no fucking shit!"

"Stop being paranoid, and let's get this over with."

"Pass the money up to her."

Nena was a ride or die chick, she loved adventure and this turned her on. She turned towards the back to retrieve the money from Rick and noticed someone walking up towards the car with a gun in their hand.

"He got a gun!"

Sean turned in time to see the guy picking up speed coming towards the car. He lifted his pistol and started shooting through the window at the approaching figure. Gun shots rang out and hit the car from the other side causing Rick to duck down on the floor. Nena was screaming as she crouched down on the front seat. Sean quickly opened his door and rolled out of it as bullets were still riddling his car. He crawled to the front of his car and noticed a body lying in front of Rick's car. The gunshots stopped. Sean held his position. All of a sudden his backdoor opened, and out jumped Rick, who looked around then decided to bolt.

He knew that it was Rick who set him up and was not about to let him get away with it. He rose up his pistol, took aim and let off two shots. One hit Rick in the upper back and the other one hit him in the lower back, lodging in his spine. Rick fell to the ground, he knew he was hit, yet he couldn't feel anything. He lay there silently, praying that he wouldn't die.

Sean knew he had to get out of there before the police arrived, or someone got his plate number. He jumped in his car. There was blood all over the front seat. Nena was laid out on the front seat. She was no longer screaming, and her eyes were closed.

"Shit!" Sean said out loud, as he started the car and pulled out. He didn't know what to do. He couldn't just dump her body, because her friend knew that she was with him. He pulled up to a red light and nervously looked over at her. He noticed that her chest kept rising.

"Thank God!" he thought to himself as he ran the light heading towards Saint Luke's hospital. Sean ran every light for six blocks until he pulled into Saint Luke's emergency room parking lot. Lifting Nena out of the car Sean rushed into the emergency room screaming, "I need a doctor!"

"She has been shot!"

"Help!"

The nurse at the station instantly instructed an orderly to get a gurney. The orderly took off and returned with a gurney. The emergency room doctor and another nurse helped the orderly take Nena from Sean and placed her on the gurney. After they took her away the nurse turned to Sean and said, "Sir I'm going to need to ask you some questions."

Sean knew that he could not stay around and end up being questioned by the police. He told the nurse, "Let me go and park my car correctly, and I will come back and answer all of your questions." The nurse started to protest, but Sean was already headed through the double doors.

He quickly jumped in his car and pulled off. He knew that he had to get his car off of the streets. He reached for his phone, but found that it was no longer there.

"Fuck it." He said out loud.

Sean decided to park his car in his mother's garage until he could figure out what to do.

8

Back in Morris Black, there was straight chaos. The homicide detectives were searching for any witnesses, the family members were screaming, and the paramedics were tending to Rick. Tone was laid out with a white sheet over his body. He got shot in the eye when Sean started shooting through the window. The bullet entered through his right eye and exited through the back of his head.

Rick was on a stretcher. The paramedics were trying to stabilize him. He was showing good vital signs, but he had no feeling from the neck down. His eyes were just roaming left to right, taking in his surroundings. The paramedics loaded him into the ambulance and headed for the hospital with lights flashing and sirens blaring. There was no rush with Tone. After the CSI finished with the crime scene, the coroner loaded his body and headed for the morgue.

Man stood watching the scene from a window on the third floor. He didn't know how he was going to explain to his aunt what had happened to Tone. His mother and aunt were both down at the scene, crying and screaming hysterically.

He reflected back, watching the scene unfold in his head. He saw Tone come out of the building, so he stepped out of the car. He was waiting for Tone to make his move, when all of a sudden gunshots rang out as Tone approached the car. He instantly drew his gun, and started firing at the car. He took off in Tone's direction. Right before his eyes he witnessed Tone take a bullet to the face and go down. Instinctively, Man unloaded the rest of his clip into the car, as he fled the scene. Now he regrets letting Rick get them involved in this, and is nervously trying to figure out how he could keep from being linked to what took place.

☐

D-Nut and Crazy were on the freeway, heading down the way.

"When you're after regular cars, the suburbs is cool, but when you want hooked up cars the inner city is where you go." Crazy tells D-Nut.

"Yeah, but you going down to the projects, them niggas pack heat."

"Nigga stop acting scary, we go catch a nigga slipping and take it to him."

"Now fire up that Skinny Minny and let's get wet." Crazy said to D-Nut as he cranked his music all the way up.

9

The courts were packed. Big Dame did it right. He is from up in Rainbow Terrace, but sees the Valley and Rainbow Terrace as being one project. Dame came up strong in the dope game. He is considered a baller, to most people. So he does what ballers do … splurge. He put up all the money to sponsor this event, which included hiring a DJ, buying refreshments, paying for the jerseys and hiring the officials to referee the game.

There were people of all ages and from all over the city in attendance. The Valley and Rainbow Terrace assembled a team of their best combined athletes. There were five starters and five subs. Disco, who is 6' 2" with crazy hops, was the starting forward. Jerry was 5' 8" with sick dribbling skills, and was the starting point guard. Oscar, who is also 5' 8", was the shooting guard. He had a wicked set shot. Then there is Yattee, who at 6' 1" played forward. Lastly there was Darrin, who stood at 6' 4" he would play center. Darrin loved to dunk on people, and sometimes this became a problem. Some people took offense to the way that he dunked on them, which has led to many fights. The starting five were on the court with their subs doing layup drills.

Andre Johnson was the DJ. He had all of his equipment out there and was cranking out the jams. It was a beautiful day. The sun was out and there was not a cloud in the sky. The temperature was 78 degrees. Girls were out in everything, from miniskirts to shorts that had their ass cheeks hanging out. Little kids were having dance competitions.

All of a sudden it sounded like thunder was approaching. There was a loud rumbling that kept getting closer. People turned in the direction from which the noise was coming. As the rumbling sound became closer, they could tell that it was bass from music. However, it's too much bass to be coming from one car. The whole block sounded like the inside of a disco hall.

A convoy of cars turned onto the street, making it evident where the noise was coming from. From the lead car, which was a 745 BMW to the last car which was a Lexus truck, all their driver doors were open. Each car door was filled with speakers that were blasting Young Jeezy's song *Go Gettas* almost in sync.

Each car had several passengers, most of which were either hanging out the windows or the sun roofs. There were fifteen cars in the caravan. There wasn't any room to park on the street, so when the lead car pulled up on the sidewalk the rest of the cars followed suite.

The Valley had an elite group of girls that ran together. These girls are what you would call high maintenance, and only fucked with ballers. They were standing together by a gold Range Rover. The Range Rover belonged to Spud, who is one of the valley girls as they referred themselves to. Spud was a red bone, who had green eyes and a body that most women would kill for. The other four girls in the click were just as fine. Their names were Robin, Monique, Nanky and Clarrisa. They were there because they knew a lot of ballers were going to be there. They were always looking for a come up, and nothing beyond pulling robberies. This click was like a pack of pit bulls in skirts.

Robin spoke, "Damn those niggas pulled up flossing."

"Them Longwood niggas are getting paper girl!" stated Monique.

"I want to get that guy, Spank." Nanky chimed in.

"Bitch, you know Spud used to fuck with him." Monica told her.

Spud jumped in, "She can have that nigga, he ain't shit but a trick, with his freaky ass."

"Tell them girl, we pass niggas around, the same way they pass bitches around." Nanky boasted.

"Look bitches, we ain't here for pleasure, we here for business, we here to see which one of these niggas can be a lick, so stay focused." Spud told them.

Clarrisa finally spoke up, "I just hope these niggas don't get to acting crazy."

"You got that right!" Robin replied.

All of the Longwood people started exiting their cars, heading for the courts. Spank and Tink were leading the pack. Spank was searching through the crowd looking for Big Dame. They were both responsible for their factions.

"Big Dame!" he called out after spotting him over by the official's table. Big Dame looked up and smiled. He started making his way towards Spank. They met up in the middle of the court they both reached out to shake hands.

"What's up, dawg!" Dame said.

"Ready to get this game going, so I can win all y'all money?" Spank asked with a laugh.

"I hear you dawg. Let's get the team captains together, so that we can go over all the rules and pass out the jerseys."

"I'm the captain of my team." responded Spank.

"Always the one to be in control huh, I like that."

"So who is the captain for the Valley?"

"It's Disco."

"Alright, let's get it going." Spank said cheerily.

Dame turned and called for Disco to come over to the courts. Disco walked over and spoke, "What's up Spank?"

Spank only answered by giving a head nod. He never really liked Disco. They often clashed on the court, because they both played very physically. Dame spoke up, "Look we hired three referees that are registered with park and rec. They are going to apply college rules. Now we are trying to have a good game. Tell your players to respect all calls made by the refs. Any arguing with the refs is going to be a tech the first time. The second time, calls for ejection. Any players that get into a heated argument or engage in physical altercations will be automatically ejected. So relay that to all of your players and one last thing Longwood y'all got the red jerseys and the Valley has blue." Dame told them.

Disco and Spank both agreed, then took off back to their teams. Spank approached the Longwood crowd and noticed that Sean wasn't present.

"Aye, Tink you ain't seen Sean?" Spank asked.

"Nope!"

"He should have been here."

"Man, call that nigga's phone and see where the hell he's at." Tink pulled out his phone and dialed Sean's number. It rung then went straight to voice mail. He tried it two more times getting the same results.

"Yo! Spank, this nigga's shit keeps going to voice mail."

"Fuck!"

"He know what's up. He's the starting point guard and is somewhere fucking around. Tink tell that nigga Pep I said he starting in Sean's spot."

The players got assigned bench areas. The Longwood players were put on the left side of the court, and the Valley were placed on the right side of the court. Most of their supporters stood in their bench areas. Dame grabbed the microphone and informed the teams that they had twenty minutes until game time so start warming up. Spank called for his team to come to the court to start running drills. The Valley team was already on the court, lined up shooting jumpers.

Ron, Bobby and Mike pulled up to the courts. Bobby blurted out, "Damn! This shit live as hell, there's bitches everywhere." Ron immediately wanted to know who he had to talk to about playing on the Valley's team.

"I can't believe that the niggas didn't invite me to play on the team, knowing I'm one of the best down here."

"They probably felt that you be on to much bullshit." Bobby responded.

"Man, fuck that! I'm going to holla at Big Dame." Ron stated as he took off looking for Dame.

Stacey's phone rang and Derrick answered it, "Who dis?"

"This Tee, I'm outside."

"Okay, I will be right out." He called out to Stacey, and told her he was leaving.

"Boy, don't forget what I said. I'm serious." Derrick just shook his head, laughed and headed out the door. He approached Tee's car and got in. As soon as he closed the door, it became hard for him to breathe. He coughed and said, "What the fuck is you burning in here?"

"Nigga this that purple haze, that real shit my nigga." Tee was high as hell. He felt like he was driving a spaceship as he pulled off. He turned to Derrick and said "It's a half a blunt in the ashtray, fire it up if you think you can handle it lil' nigga."

"Look, I know you high, but watch who you calling a lil' nigga. You know I handle mines." Tee liked Derrick, because he knew that he had heart and wasn't going to back down for anything. So he said, "My bad fire it up nigga."

"That's more like it, now let me blaze this shit up!" Derrick said as he lit the blunt.

10

Hey Dame!" Ron said.

"That's fucked up man!"

"What's fucked up?"

"That y'all ain't letting me be on the team."

"Man, you be in and out of jail so much, we couldn't count on you."

"Well I'm here right now, so what's up, is y'all go let me play or what?"

"Look we got the starters, but we do need an extra sub, so if you want to come off the bench, go holla at Disco."

"Alright bet, I just want to stunt on them niggas. I know they can't stop me." Ron said, as he walked in Disco's direction. Spank had his Team in a huddle, "Look y'all we can beat these niggas. That shit last year was a fluke. Listen I got ten stacks on this game, so please keep y'all head. If we win, I got y'all." he explained to his players.

On the other end of the court Disco had his teammates together, giving them the same type of pep talk, "Y'all know we smashed those niggas last year, and we can do it again this year. Big Dame got gees on us, plus he paid for this whole event, so let's not let him down. Now Ron go be playing with us. He go be subbing for Oscar. So are we all on the same page?" everybody nodded in agreement.

"Alright the starting five take the floor and everyone else to the bench." he informed them.

The ref blew the whistle, signaling the start of the game. All the players came to the center of the court, for the tip off. Spank and Darrin were in the circle, ready to try to take control of the tip. The ref blew the whistle, and then tossed the ball up in the air. They jumped, Spank hit it to Mac. The game began with Longwood having first possession.

☐

Sean's mother was at work, so he had time to do what he needed to do. He pulled his car into the garage and closed the door. Inside was a door that led into the house, he entered and went straight to the phone. He had to make two important calls. First he called two-tone Dave. He told him that he needed him to come get his car, to do bodywork, paint it and replace the windows. He told him that it was urgent, and that he needed him to shoot through right at that moment. Dave told him that he was on his way.

Dave could be trusted because he had a car repair shop that also served as a chop shop, so he is real discreet. Next he tried calling Spank to let him know what went down. He got no answer and figured it was because of the game. Next he dialed Tink's phone. Tink answered, "Who dis?"

"Tink its Sean!"

"Nigga where you at? Spank tripping!"

"Man that punk ass nigga Rick from Morris Black set me up. I had to lay him and another nigga down. I had a bitch with me and she got hit up, it's all bad!"

"So where are you at now?"

"I'm at my mother's. I'm waiting on Two-Tone Dave to come get my car."

"Did you get hit, and did they get the shit?"

"No, I'm good. I still got the shit, plus the faggot ass nigga dropped the money in my car."

"So what do you need me to do?"

"I need you to get somebody to go up to Saint Luke's and check on Nena. I think her last name is Miles. Somebody has to make sure that she is alright and that she doesn't talk to the police, or at least doesn't mention my name."

"Alright, I'm going to send Coco up there. Do you want me to have someone come and get you?"

"No, my nerves are bad I think I'm going to lay low for a minute."

"Okay, I'll let Spank know what's up, and send Coco to handle that."

"Thanks Tink." Sean told him then hung up.

Tink walked over to the sidewalk where Coco's truck was parked. Coco, Silvia and Renee were each sipping on a bottle of corona.

"Coco let me holla at you for a minute!"

"What's up boo?" she asked as she gave him a hug.

"I need you to do me a favor. There is a girl that Sean had with him who got shot and is up at Saint Luke's. Her name is Nena Miles. I need you to go up there, and see if she is okay and that she doesn't mention Sean's name in any way."

"I got you boo. It's just ironic, how when I got pulled over by that cops on my way up here, my excuse for speeding was that I was on my way to the hospital. Now here I am really on my way up there." She thought for a minute then asked, "Do you want me to leave them here or take them with me?"

"That's up to you."

"Okay, then I'm gone." She walked back over to her truck and told her girls, "I got to take care of some business, do y'all want to roll or stay here until I get back?"

"Bitch, we came with you, so we are leaving with you." Renee said.

"Okay, let's roll!"

Tink walked back over to the courts. Spank was down low with the ball, when a ref blew the whistle signaling a timeout. Spank angrily walked over to the bench.

"Who the fuck called a timeout?"

"I was about to take that nigga."

"I called a time out, to put you up on what happened to Sean." Tink explained.

"It better be important."

"It is they tried to rob him up in Morris Black. He just called me, saying that he had to lay a couple niggas down, and that the girl that was with him got shot."

"I told that nigga, I couldn't believe that Rick had enough money to buy a bird. So where is he at now?" The ref blew the whistle, signaling that the timeout was over. Spank yelled for Meechie to go in for him. Then Tink answered, "He says he's at his mother's house. He said his car got shot up, and that he's trying to lay low. I sent Coco up to Saint Luke's to see if the girl is okay and to make sure that she don't mention his name."

"Call that nigga, so I can holla at him."

Tink scrolled through his phone until he found the number, then he hit the call button and handed the phone to Spank.

Sean answered, "Hello?"

"Nigga I told you that it sounded like some bullshit!" Spank yelled into the phone.

"I ain't trying to hear that shit right now."

"Your right, my bad, listen we are going to handle this shit. You just sit tight. As soon as this game is over with, I'm going to shoot up there and holla at you. You know it's nothing but love." Spank told him.

"Thanks, you know you're my dawg."

"Okay let me get back to this game. Keep your head up." Spank told him then handed the phone back to Tink.

"So what's up?" Tink asked.

"Shit, we got to play it by ear. When you hear from Coco, let me know what's up. I'm about to get back to this game."

11

Fred was hyped. He was driving his 1973 drop top Cutlass, that was sitting on 24" Daytons. He had four fifteens mounted in his trunk, and the doors had eight mid-range speakers in them. He had just gotten his car washed and waxed earlier that day. He was also dressed to impress. He had on an all Polo outfit and a pair of Jordans. He was at 73rd and Kinsman, and the courts were on the next street.

Doc was sitting in the passenger's seat, smoking a Dutch. He knew that a lot of girls were going to be up there, and couldn't wait to put his game down. Ronald was in the back seat, all smiles. He was just happy to be in the mix. He usually gets left out when they attend big events because he was like a third leg, he couldn't pull no hoes.

Fred made a left on 75th street and couldn't believe how crowded the street was. People were everywhere. They were on both sides of the streets. There were groups of people standing on porches. Fred was feeling like a superstar, cruising down the block. He was looking for a place to park, but the street and the sidewalk were full.

"Park up the hill and we can walk back down." Ronald said.

"Nigga is you crazy? This ain't your raggedy shit. You think I'm going to leave my shit for somebody to take it? You know how these niggas are down here."

Ronald got offended, "Boy, my shit ain't raggedy."

"Matter of fact let me out right here I'll be at the courts when you find a spot." Doc was anxious to get to the bitches and jumped in, "I'm going to roll with him Fred."

Fred couldn't believe that those niggas were thirsty like that.

"Fuck it! Get y'all asses out, punk ass niggas."

"Don't be mad at us because you ain't got a place to park your shit." Ronald said to him, as him and Doc got out of the car. Fred just drove off. He was contemplating calling Shannon, to see if he could park at her house, but he really wasn't trying to fuck with her. He was trying to come up on some new pussy, so he turned back onto the avenue.

☐

Crazy seen a blue drop top Cutlass, pull onto the avenue and turned to D-Nut.

"Look at that pretty mother fucker right there." D-Nut turned and saw the car.

"We can get that!"

"When he stops at the light I'm going to bump him, and when he steps out to confront me you get out and creep up on him."

"I got you!" replied D-Nut.

Fred pulled up to a red light, and his car was hit from the back. He cursed, threw his car in park and got out. He went to the back to inspect the damage. Crazy stepped out of his car and walked towards Fred, with an apologetic look on his face. At the same time D-Nut climbed out of the car and crouched down. Fred was looking at his taillight, which was busted when Crazy approached him.

"My fault, my brakes have been tripping lately. I got to get them fixed."

"You're driving real reckless."

"Look I got insurance, just let me grab the information right quick and we can take care of it." Crazy walked back to his car, and Fred walked back towards his to grab a pen. He opened his passenger's door, and then opened up the glove compartment. D-Nut crept up on him and said, "What's up crab?" Fred looked up and seen a big gun in his face. He stood up, "What's going on?"

"Nigga this a jack move, beat it!" Fred was mad at his self for slipping. His gun was in the car under the seat. He thought to himself, "I ain't going out like no sucker."

He faked like he was about to walk away, but quickly turned and went for D-Nut's gun. He wasn't fast enough, and D-Nut shot him through the hand. When Fred turned and started running, D-Nut kept shooting. He shot Fred in the leg as he ran between two houses. Fred fell to the ground after a few minutes passed he pulled his self up and hobbled back towards the courts.

After shooting Fred, D-Nut jumped in the car and pulled off with Crazy following him.

12

Tee and Derrick were sitting in the car, high as hell. The purple haze had them floating on cloud nine. They had been parked at the courts for about twenty minutes. They had finished the half a blunt that was left in the ashtray, then lit up another one. They were too high to even pay attention to the game.

Tee was tripping, talking to himself, "Bitch ass trying to play me, I ain't no sucker, I'm going to fuck his bitch ass up."

Derrick looked over, "Man, what are you talking about?"

"That nigga Ron, I'm going to fuck him up as soon as I see him."

"I told you that he was going to be up here. You aren't going to see him sitting in here."

"You're right, let me get focused."

He reached under his seat and pulled out a 40 glock and tucked it in his waist. He got out of the car, and almost fell because he was so high. He leaned on the car for support. Derrick got out of the car and took in all the sights. He looked and seen Ron on the court dribbling the ball.

"There go Ron right there."

"Where?" Tee asked as he tried to focus in on the court.

"Right there with the number three jersey on." Once Tee made Ron out, he staggered towards the court. The game was back in full progress. Longwood was advancing the ball, with Ron checking Mac, who had the ball at the top of the key. Tee walked right onto the court. People started wondering what was going on. A ref tried to stop him only to be pushed to the ground.

People started yelling, "Get off the court!"

The players were oblivious to what was going on. Mac shot a jumper, and missed. Ron rushed to crash the back board for the rebound. He never made it back to his feet. As he was coming down with the ball, Tee hit him with a blow to his jaw. Ron fell to the ground, hitting his head in the process.

The Valley teammates rushed over to help him, but stopped when they saw that Tee had pulled out a big gun. Tee started pistol whipping Ron while yelling, "Where is my money, nigga?" Ron was out cold. Derrick called to Tee, "Come on man, it ain't worth it. Get out of here before somebody calls the police."

Tee just stood there for a minute, still feeling the effects of the haze. He then looked down at Ron laying there unconscious. As he turned away to leave, he doubled back and kicked Ron hard to the chest as he mumbled, "Bitch ass nigga!" He then started back towards his car.

Everyone was clearing his path, wanting no part of him or the big gun that he was carrying. Once Tee left the court, people rushed over to help Ron. Someone yelled, "Call an ambulance!" A girl that was sitting on her porch when it happened ran in her house and got a pillow. She made her way over to him, and put the pillow under his head. He was breathing but he was still unconscious. The girl whispered to him, "Hold on baby, you're going to be okay."

The Longwood players were all at their bench, as were the Valley players. Each was talking about how what had just happened was messed up. Spank felt no sympathy. To him that was an everyday occurrence.

"Dude must have gotten what he had coming." he thought as he went in search of Big Dame. He found him standing over Ron, and told him, "Just move him off of the court, so that we can finish the game."

"We can't do that!"

"So you saying we got to wait to finish the game?"

"We don't know what's all wrong with him, and I'm not try-ing to mess him up any worse. The people are on their way, and after they take him off the court we can resume the game." Dame said as he heavily sighed. Spank was pissed, but he knew that there wasn't anything that he could do, so he walked back over to the benches.

13

Fred saw some people sitting on a porch, and limped in their direction. The people looked up as he approached, and seen blood on his hand and leg as well as the look of pain on his face. The old lady, whose name was Mrs. Pearl asked him, "Boy what happened to you?"

"I got carjacked and shot, could you call an ambulance for me?"

"This doesn't make any damn sense. What is this world coming to!" she said more to herself than anybody else. She called out to her sons, "John, Mikey, y'all help that boy up here, and bring him into the house." They helped Fred into the house and were about to sit him in a chair, when Mrs. Pearl yelled, "Hold up, get some plastic. I don't want that boy getting blood all over my furniture."

She picked up the phone and called 911. She had been living in the Valley for over 25 years. She had lost her husband to cancer and two sons to violence. She had two sons left and vowed to try her hardest to keep them out of harm's way. She knew that the projects were unsafe, but living on a fixed income she couldn't afford to move to a better neighborhood. While she was on the phone, she heard an ambulance zoom by her house. Hearing the sirens she turned to Fred. "Are you sure that you were the only one that got hurt?"

"Yes ma'am."

She called out to Mikey, "Boy step outside and see where that thing is going." Mikey stepped out onto the porch, and looked in the direction that the ambulance was going. He saw that it was parked in the middle of the street in front of the courts. He went back into the house and said, "Ma something must have happened at the courts, because that's where the ambulance is parked."

"Lord I will be glad when I can get away from this place. This is just madness. Mikey go down there and tell them people, that it's another person injured down here. Ain't no telling when another one of them things will come this way?" Mikey took off towards the courts.

There were three paramedics attending to Ron, who was still unconscious. First they set his neck with a brace. Then they laid a wooden gurney next to him. The crowd had closed in around them so much, that there was hardly any room for them to work. One of the paramedics stood up and said, "Step back please, we need room!" Dame grabbed the microphone and urged everybody to move back. The crowd backed up, making room.

Mikey pushed through the crowd. Once he reached the paramedics, he caught his breath, and then said, "Excuse me but there is a person that has been shot at my house down the street!"

"Sorry sir, but we are only allowed to deal with one call at a time." one of the paramedics informed him. He then asked Mikey for his address and assured him that he would radio dispatch and make sure that another ambulance would be sent to his address. Mikey told him, "Thanks!" and took off back towards his house. When he got back, he told his mother what the paramedic said, and her response was, "Jesus that's why so many black folks die, we can't ever get any medical assistance when we need it."

Fred asked her if she could call his friend that stayed up the street. He explained that she had a car and would drive him to the hospital. Truth be told he wanted to keep what happened to him on the low. He gave the number to Mrs. Pearl, and she put the phone to his ear, Shannon answered. After he told her what happened he gave her the address and waited for her to arrive.

☐

Coco arrived at Saint Luke's, and approached the emergency room window.

"I would like to know if y'all have admitted a Nena Miles?"

"Let me check." said the nurse as she started typing into the computer.

The nurse looked up, "Are you related to her?"

"Yes she is my sister."

"And your name is?"

"Carmella Miles."

"Well Ms. Miles, she has been admitted. She is in surgery right now."

"How bad is she?"

"She suffered a gunshot wound to her right chest. You will have to talk to the doctor to find out any more information."

"So when can I see the doctor?"

"Like I said they are in surgery right now, and I do not know how much longer they will be in there. You can wait if you want, and as soon as he is finished I will inform him that you wish to speak to him."

"Thank you." Coco said and she walked outside to call Tink. She dialed his number, "Hello?"

"Baby, I'm up here at the hospital, and they said that she got shot in the chest, and is in surgery. The nurse told me that I would have to wait for the doctor to find out what her condition is. So do you want me to wait or what?"

"Yeah stay up there and holla at the doctor. As soon as she is able to talk I want you there."

"Okay baby."

"One more thing have the police been up there asking questions?"

"I haven't seen any police since I got here."

"Alright, keep me updated, I'm gone." Tink hung up and walked over to Spank, who was still fuming about the delay in the game.

"Spank I just talked to Coco, and she said that old girl got hit in the chest and is in surgery right now but she said she ain't seen no police up there. She is going to wait to talk to the doctor, to see what's up with her."

"That's what's up. Let me go and holla at Dame. I see the ambulance has got here." Spank walks over to Dame.

"How much longer will it be?"

"They are taking him right now, so it shouldn't be that much longer." Spank started walking back towards the bench, when someone called his name. He turned and seen Nanky who was Spud's friend standing there. He walked in her direction, and started thinking about how she used to flirt with him. She had a banging body, and some lips that were made for dick sucking.

"What's up ma?"

"Nothing much just bored."

"I feel you, I'm about to go and sit in my car and smoke a blunt."

"Can I smoke with you?"

"Of course, anything else would be uncivilized." They took off headed for his car. Once inside, Spank rolled up his windows which were tinted. He then fired up a blunt, hit it a couple of times then passed it to Nanky. While she was hitting it, he pulled his dick out of his shorts. Nanky looked at him like he was crazy.

"Boy what are you doing?"

"Don't front baby girl, you know you been at a nigga. I'm stressing right now, so handle this and I got you."

"Just like that?" she asked.

"Just like that." he said as he took the blunt from her with one hand, while using the other hand to guide her face to his dick. She did not even protest. He put the blunt in the ash tray, and grabbed his dick. He held one hand to the back of her head. She could only take him in so far. Spank started pushing her head down further, and his legs started to cramp. He told her, "Hold up ma." She rose up and he hit the seat controls. He put the seat back as far as it would go, then put it in the reclining position. Nanky did not need any more persuasion. She reached over and grabbed his dick, then lowered her head. Spank just laid back, and watched his dick going in and out of her mouth. Spud was a freak bitch, so he figured that any bitch that hung with her had to be a freak too. As he reached down to grab her hair, he said to himself, "I guess I figured right." Nanky thought that if she gave him that good head, that she was known for, that she could get all the way in with him.

She thought that sex, was all men's weak point. She had been using sex since she was fifteen, to get what she wanted. She was molested by a family friend when she was younger. To keep her quiet he used to shower her with money and gifts. As she got older, she found out that most men would do anything for good sex. She was using her best skills on Spank. She sucked his balls, jacked him off, deep throated him and let him cum in her mouth until it was dripping out from the corner of her lips. She used her sleeve to wipe it off, that disgusted Spank. He reached over his sun visor and took down a wad of money and peeled off $50.00 and threw it in her lap.

"What is this for?"

"For your services baby girl."

"Spank you got me fucked up! You can't play me like that."

"Baby girl you played yourself. Now let's go, I got to get back to this game."

"You ain't shit Spank!"

"So I have heard." He replied smiling as he walked back towards the court.

Nanky felt humiliated, as she walked back towards Spud's truck. She couldn't believe that he played her like that. When she got to the truck, Robin asked, "Bitch where you have been?"

"I was hollering at Spank's trick ass. The nigga offered me three hundred dollars to go to the hotel with him."

"And what did you say?"

"I told him to give me five."

"And what did he say?" questioned Spud.

"He asked for my number, and told me that he would call me."

Spud knew that she was lying. Spank was a freak, but he wasn't a trick. Spud knew this first hand, because she had started off trying to get him to trick with her and ended up playing herself. He ended up dogging her, then cutting her off. To save face, she started telling people that he was a trick. Truth be told he never gave her any money, plus she had fell for him. She caught feelings, and was hurt when he cut her off. She knew that Nanky was lying, but felt that it was not the time to bust her out.

When Spank got back to the court, the paramedics were loading Ron into the ambulance.

"Now we can get this thing going." He said to himself.

Dame got on the mic, "The game will resume after the court has been cleaned." He had sent a youngster to the corner store to get some bleach and rags, so that they could clean up the blood that was left on the court by Ron. The Longwood side of the court was clean, so spank told his players to start warming back up.

Disco was on the other end talking to his team, "Look y'all, we got to stay focused. Do not let what happened to Ron take y'all off your game. So let's get out there and beat these niggas."

Shannon arrived at Mrs. Pearl's house, before the ambulance did. Mikey walked out of the house and brought her inside. Fred was sitting in a chair at the kitchen table. His hand and leg were both wrapped in towels. Mrs. Pearl spoke, "Child, you better get this boy to the hospital before he bleeds to death. It's a shame I called that damn thing forty five minutes ago." She told her son's to help Fred. As they were putting him in the car, an ambulance pulled onto the street. Shannon asked, "What do you want to do?"

"They took too long, you can take me."

"Yeah, but they can give you the medical attention that you need right now. You done lost a lot of blood. Let them take you and I will follow." Fred reluctantly agreed, and the paramedics loaded him into the ambulance. They pulled off with Shannon following them.

She didn't really know what was going on, but she was going to stand by him. She knew that he only looked at her as a jump off, but she really did care about him. She thought that it was a good time to tell him she was six weeks pregnant. She had been holding off telling him because she didn't know how he would react. Maybe it would encourage him to get his life together.

Shannon had finished four years of college and had a good job. If it wasn't for her insecurities she could have had any man that she chose. Since middle school she had been attracted to bad boys, and she has never out grown that. Her mother couldn't understand her choice in men, and neither could she. She really cared for Fred, and wanted to have his baby, so she decided to tell him that she was pregnant as soon as he gets released from the hospital.

☐

Man was at his aunt's house, talking to his family. Tone's mother wanted to know what happened. The Homicide Department could not provide her with any information, because they could not find one witness. Even if someone saw what happened, they knew that coming forward would lead to retaliation. The code in the Black, was what happens in the streets gets dealt with in the streets.

Tone's mother did not care about any street code. Her only son was dead and she wanted to know why, so she turned to Man for answers.

The story that he was telling her was far from the truth. He told her that Rick was supposed to be copping some work from a nigga name Sean from Longwood, but that it was a set up. He told her that Sean and someone else tried to rob Rick, and when he and Tone tried to step in that they started shooting.

She yelled, "That wasn't any of y'all business. Everybody knows that Rick is no good. He is always into something, and now my baby is gone. Y'all just get out! Get out!" They headed out the door.

Tone's mother could not figure out where it all went wrong. She got pregnant when she was fifteen, and had to raise him by herself. His father was an older man that was married at the time and became a deadbeat dad. She made sure that Tone never wanted for anything, so she didn't understand why he chose the streets. By his early teens he had done multiple juvenile stints. As an adult, he did two bids for robbery and assault. With all of his shortcomings, she felt that he still did not deserve to die. She wanted to see whoever killed her son brought to justice, be it through the judicial system or through the streets.

Man and three other boys were outside. There was Tez, Ray-Ray and Jerrel. They were all cousins, and they loved gun play. They had been riding with and for each other since they were kids. They were younger than Tone and Man, so they looked up to them.

"What's up cousin? What are we going to do? You know we got to ride for Tone." Ray Ray said.

"I fuck with this chick named Linda that lives down in Longwood. I'm going to get up with her, and have her put me down on where the nigga lay his head at."

"Keep us posted cuz. You know we are ready to ride." said Tez. The three of them gave Man dap, then left.

15

Saint Luke's hospital was very busy. Rick was in the trauma unit. The bullet that hit him in the spine cracked his vertebrae damaging his nerves. He was paralyzed from the neck down. The hospital was waiting for a specialist to arrive to perform surgery. Removing the bullet could cause more damage or even death. Rick was conscious, but wished that he was dreaming. The reality was that he may never walk again. Silently tears rolled down his cheeks.

On the third floor was Ron, and he was in even worse condition. He was in a coma. The blows to his head caused swelling in his brain. The doctor was working to relieve the pressure. He could possibly suffer permanent brain damage, if he recovered.

Down in the emergency room, Fred was being tended to. He was very lucky that both bullets went straight through without causing any major damage. He was ready to be released, with only some bandages and a pair of crutches. Before he could leave, two detectives came to visit him. They first inquired about how he had received the gunshots. He explained to them, that he had been carjacked. Not believing his story they went on to question him about a shooting up in Morris Black. He told them, that he knew nothing about it, but that his car was missing. In response, they told him that they only dealt with homicides and violent crimes, and to have a nice day.

Nena was finally out of surgery and placed in recovery. The doctor had been informed that there were family members waiting to learn her status. Coco approached the doctor, "Hi, I am Nena Miles sister, and I would like to know what condition she is in?"

"Well Ms. Miles your sister has a collapsed lung that we had to repair. She is listed in critical but stable condition."

"When will she be able to talk?"

"Because of the lung and tubes that are placed in her throat, she may not be able to talk for at least a couple of weeks."

"When can I see her?"

"You won't be allowed to see her until tomorrow morning." Coco figured there wasn't anything else that she could do, so she called Tink, gave him the update and told him that she was on her way back down there. When she got to her truck, Silvia and Renee were both asleep.

"Y'all bitches wake up!" she yelled as she climbed in her truck.

"Damn bitch, you was in that place forever!" said Silvia.

"They still had her in surgery. She is out now, but they won't let me see her until tomorrow. So we are headed back down to the Valley."

"Bout time, I'm trying to see what them big, black, sweaty niggas are working with." stated Renee.

Silvia chimed in, "Girl you are so nasty."

Coco spoke up "Silvia ... bitch fire that blunt up, and let me put my music back on. I'm not going to let the rest of my day be spoiled behind some bitch that I don't even know. Sean is cool, but he needs to handle his own business."

"Girl I know that's right" Silvia stated. They cranked the music, smoked the blunt, and talked shit as they headed back to the Valley.

16

Sean was still at his mother's house. Dave had come and picked up his car, and promised to keep the situation a secret. His mother entered the house and was shocked to see him there because she did not see his car parked outside. He has always been a momma's boy, and his mother knew when something was bothering him.

"Boy why do you look like somebody just died?

He tried to lie, "Ain't nothing wrong." But she also knows when he is lying.

"Boy I know that something is going on with you. Why couldn't you just stay in school? You are too smart to be throwing your life away." Sean had heard it all before, and wasn't trying to hear it again. So he thought of something to get her off of his back.

"I crashed my car and the person that was with me got hurt."

"How bad?" He hated lying to his mother but he knew that he could not tell her the truth about what happened.

"She broke her leg."

"Is your insurance going to cover it?"

"Don't worry ma," he told her as he headed into the bedroom. He realized that he still hadn't heard back from Tink, so he decided to call him back.

"What's up?"

"This is Sean, have you heard anything yet?"

"Yeah my nigga, Coco just left from up there. She said old girl had a collapsed lung, but they fixed it. She's in critical but stable condition, and she can't see her until tomorrow."

"What about Rick and the other nigga that I had to lay down, have you heard anything about them?"

"Shit, I only know what you told me. I did ask Coco if any police been up there asking questions and she said no. Far as I know you are good. You might as well come down here. I will send somebody to get you."

"Alright, send somebody to get me, because my mother is driving me crazy."

"Bet," said Tink as he hung up. He walked over to the benches and called for Allen.

"Al I need you to go and pick up Sean from his mother's house."

"She still stay on Dove right?"

"Yeah, the first house on the left side of the street."

Allen got in his car and pulled off. He was a loyal soldier, and he was a rider. When he was younger he had nothing, not even the respect of his peers. Spank used to see him around the hood looking bummy. He would pay him to run errands, and after a while Spank took a liking to Allen. Once Spank came up in the game, he put Allen on his team, and for that he would always be thankful and loyal. He had put in much work for Spank, including putting niggas to sleep.

The game was back in progress. It was the third quarter, with the Valley being up by six. Spank was frustrated, because Disco was playing him with hot defense. Spank wasn't able to dominate the game. Longwood had the ball. Mac was bringing the ball down the court. Spank was down in the post, calling for the ball, and Mac passed it to him. Spank tried to back Disco down, but he wouldn't budge, so out of frustration Spank faked like he was going up and caught Disco in the jaw with his elbow. Disco bent over holding his jaw and Spank took that opportunity to take the shot. He made it, and headed back down the court. Disco got his self together, and headed back down the court also. He ran up on Spank.

"That's how we are playing now?" Spank acted dumb.

"I don't know what you're talking about."

"It's cool dawg, play ball" Disco told him as he tried to get open. Jerry had the ball with Disco going baseline Oscar set a pick on Spank. When Disco got free, Jerry threw up an alley hoop. Disco caught the ball in the air and dunked it. The crowd started going crazy. Spank was pissed, and complained to the ref that the pick was illegal.

Disco ran past, "Don't start crying now nigga." Spank went down in the post again and called for the ball. He shook Disco and blew past him, going up for a layup. Disco timed him, and came from behind blocking his shot on the back board. Again the crowd erupted. Disco egged him on, "Nigga, come hard or go home."

"Fuck your soft ass!"

"Shut up and play ball." Spank was a hero to the people from Longwood, so they did not take kindly to him being humiliated. The crowd yelled, "Dog that nigga, Spank!"

Disco told him, "I see you brought your cheerleaders. All they need is some pompoms!" then he headed up court. The Valley had the ball, and Oscar shot a jumper but missed it. Both Spank and Disco went up for the rebound, with Disco coming down with the ball.

When he went back up court, Spank stuck his foot out and tripped him. A whistle blew and the ref called a foul. Disco walked over to Spank.

"Nigga don't do that shit no more."

"What are you going to do?"

"Do some more punk shit and you are going to see."

"We might as well get it on right now!" Spank said as he walked up on him. As soon as he got within Disco's reach Spank caught one to the jaw that put him down on one knee. Before Disco could advance the ref grabbed him and people rushed the court. The other refs stood in front of Disco as the Longwood players helped Spank back to his feet. Spank stood up, "Your mine, bitch!" The ref informed them that they both had been ejected from the game.

Dame was upset, because Disco was his best player. Now it was going to be harder for them to win the game. He had lost two players. He knew that there was going to be trouble from the beginning. Every year a fight breaks out, that's why sometimes he felt that the money wasn't even worth it. Then again it wasn't even about the money, it was about giving back. Dame was born in the Valley, and even though he sold drugs, he had witnessed firsthand what the drug trade had done to his neighborhood.

He tried to give back, by sponsoring events, for the kids from his hood.

He needed to get things back under control before they got out of hand. He could not afford for a kid to get hurt behind some nonsense, so he went over to holla at Tink.

"Talk to your boy. Tell him to chill out and let's finish the game."

"I got you, I know he gets a little hotheaded."

"Don't worry we are going to finish the game." He took off to holla at Spank. He found him by the car.

"You got ten grand on this shit, use your head."

"Fuck that shit, I'm going to fuck that nigga up." The Longwood crew gathered around and Spank stepped up.

"What's up Spank? We will tear this bitch up just give the word."

Tink got mad, "Y'all niggas chill!" then he turned to Spank.

"See the nigga after the game, at least finish it."

"Alright, you got that my nigga." With Disco and Spank off the court, the game resumed. Disco was on the sideline, mad at his self. He had just told his teammates to stay focused, then he let Spank bitch ass, take him out of his hook up. He knew that his actions might cost Dame the game, so he went in search of him to apologize.

Dame seen him coming his way, "Don't even sweat it, shit happens."

"He was playing real dirty, Dame. He was trying to hurt me."

"He knows now that you ain't a chump. We can still win. I just need you to help Duck out with the coaching."

"You got that" replied Disco as he took off towards the coach.

17

Tee and Derrick left the courts, and went and copped two more blunts. Tee spent his last forty dollars, and he felt stupid. He fucked Ron up, but didn't even check his pockets to see if he had some money. He was buzzing and having crazy thoughts. He said to his self fuck it and headed towards the freeway. Derrick noticed the direction in which they were headed and asked, "Where are we going?"

"I got to make a withdrawal right quick." He jumped on the freeway, and headed towards Lakewood. He exited the freeway, on the west side of town, then drove three blocks and pulled into a First Merit bank parking lot. He told Derrick that he would be right back and left the car running.

Derrick turned the music up, setback in the seat and continued to smoke the blunt.

Tee entered the bank and headed straight towards a female teller. The security guard did not even pay him any attention when he walked in.

When he reached the teller she asked, "May I help you?"

"I have a gun and if you do any of the following three things I will kill you. One, make any noise. Two, try to press the alarm and three try to put a dye pack in the money. Do you understand me?" The teller shook her head saying yes. He then instructed her to hand him all of the twenty, fifty and one hundred dollar bills. The teller did as she was directed. Tee stuffed some of the money in his pockets, and tucked the rest in his waist band. He then said to the teller, "If you want to live please do not make any noise until after I am gone. He then turned and headed for the door. When he reached for the door handle the teller screamed, "He just robbed me!" pointing towards Tee.

The security guard immediately drew his weapon and gave chase. Tee was two feet away from his car, when the security guard yelled, "Freeze!" Tee turned and started firing at him, and the guard returned fire. During the exchange the guard was hit high in the chest and went down. Derrick watched it all in slow motion. He was so high that he really didn't know what was going on. Tee jumped in the car and pulled out of the parking lot speeding. He thought he was in the clear, but the teller had ran to the window when the guard gave chase. She had seen the make and model of the car and the direction that it left in. She quickly called the police and gave them the information. An all-points bulletin was put out on Tee's car.

His adrenaline was pumping, as he jumped back on the freeway headed back to the east side. A State Highway patrol car that was sitting on the median, heard the call. He saw a car fitting the description speeding and driving erratically. So he pulled out and gave chase. Tee picked up speed, traveling at over a hundred miles per hour. Derrick began to sober up real fast, as realization started to set in.

"What the fuck did you do?" he yelled. Tee was not trying to talk, he would explain later. Right now he was trying to concentrate on getting away. The trooper radioed in for back up, and another cruiser got on the freeway up ahead and laid down spike strips. Tee was going over a hundred, when he hit them. Both of the front tires blew, but Tee didn't stop, he kept riding on the rims. He saw an exit up ahead and went for it.

Derrick was in a state of shock, and all he could think about were the words that Stacey kept telling him, "Stay away from Tee." They got on the west 25th Street exit ramp, with four police cars in hot pursuit. Sparks were flying from the bare rims riding on the concrete. As Tee was coming off the ramp he approached an intersection that had a traffic light. The light was red but instead of stopping he made a right turn and the car slid sideways. The car went up on the sidewalk stopping. Tee tried to make a way through oncoming traffic and crashed into a light.

Tee climbed out of the shattered window and took off. Derrick was not so lucky. He was stuck, his right leg was broken and pinned under the dash board. The police quickly surrounded the car, with their guns drawn. They had to have the fire department use the Jaws of Life to free Derrick.

Tee ran between some houses and jumped some fences. He did not even know where he was at, and his mouth was bleeding. He had lost three teeth, when his face hit the steering wheel during the impact. He came out of a backyard and saw a teenage boy and girl walking towards a car. He ran up scaring them. The girl noticed the blood spilling from his mouth and the gun in his hand, and got ready to scream. Tee raised the gun and the girl covered her mouth. Tee told the boy, "I just need a ride, I will pay you two hundred dollars." He reached in his pocket and pulled out a knot of bills, letting the kid see that he was serious. The kid's eyes lit up.

"Get in." Tee climbed into the backseat and laid down.

The kid asked him, "Where are you going?"

"Take me to the east side, once you get over there I will give you directions."

"Okay!" The kid said and took off. His girlfriend was terrified and asked could she be dropped off. Tee told her that she had to go along for the ride, but not to worry everything was going to be alright.

Back at the bank, the police were securing the crime scene and questioning the witnesses. The teller gave a description of Tee to one of the officers. The security guard was in the back of the ambulance being rushed to Metro hospital. The paramedics were working frantic to revive him. He had stopped breathing twice already and they revived him, but nothing that they were doing was bringing him back. They pulled in to the emergency room, and rushed him inside of the hospital. They continued to work on him, for forty-five minutes. After trying everything that they could they declared him dead. Derrick was now looking at an aggravated murder charge.

18

Ronald and Doc were wondering where the hell Fred was.

"You think that nigga said fuck us, and road out?" Doc asked.

"He was mad but I don't think he would leave us hanging like that."

"Call his cell phone again."

"I done called six times already. It just keeps going to voice mail."

"Let's go see if we can knock some bitches off, ain't no sense in just waiting around."

"Look at them bitches over there by that Range Rover, they are tight."

"Let the games begin!" Doc said as he walked in the direction of the Range Rover.

Spud and her girls were standing by her truck, just scoping out the scene, when they noticed two guys walking in their direction. Nanky spoke out, "I hope them bum ass niggas ain't about to try and get no holla."

"Them niggas are walking, they can't have shit." Robin said.

"Maybe they got their car parked somewhere else. Let's just see what they are talking about." Spud advised. Spud had been in the game for a while, and knows that you can't always judge a book by its cover. She had lost out on a few good licks, by solely going off a person's appearance. She smiled as they approached.

"What's up fellas?" she asked them.

"Nothing much, we just saw you beautiful ladies over here and thought that we would come and say hello." Doc told her.

"Are y'all walking?" Nanky questioned them.

Doc was taken aback by her attitude. He thought to himself there is always one in the bunch. He relayed that it's actually three of them, and that their friend was looking for a place to park. Nanky figured that the one with the car might be about something, but that those two were scrubs.

"So where are y'all from?" inquired Spud.

"We are from 116th and Buckeye" Ronald told her.

"So you know Rico?" Robin jumped in with questions.

"Which Rico?"

"Rico with the blue Benz, that be at RD's."

"Yeah I know Rico, that's my nigga" stated Ronald.

"Group meeting!" Robin said to her girls. They gathered in a huddle out of the guys ear shot.

Robin said, "Buster alert."

"Girl, what are you talking about?" inquired Nanky.

"Bitch, the boys are fake, I made that shit up, about a nigga named Rico with the Benz."

"Girl, you lying!" said Spud, as they all busted out laughing. They broke the huddle, and Spud told them, "It was nice meeting y'all, but we got to make a move."

Doc asked, "Well can we at least get a number or something?"

"I don't think that would be a good idea!" Spud told him, as she climbed in her truck. Doc and Ronald stood there baffled, as the rest of the girls got in the truck. Spud started the truck, and Nanky rolled her window down, and yelled, "Busters!"

Ronald yelled back, "Eat a dick bitch!"

Nanky replied, "If you had one." as they pulled off laughing.

"I wonder what those hoes are tripping about." said Ronald.

"Nigga! Who the fuck is Rico with the blue Benz?" Doc asked him.

"Shit, I don't know."

"Those hoes probably knew that your ass was lying. You made us look like some cold chumps. From now on you let me do the talking."

"Man fuck those bitches, let's go find Fred." Together they walked back towards the courts.

Allen picked Sean up, and they were headed back to the Valley. Allen tried to start a conversation, "You cool dawg? I heard you was in a little gun play." Sean didn't know how much he could trust him, so he just said, "I'm good." Allen figured that it would be best to just let him be.

They pulled up to the courts. Allen pulled back up on the sidewalk to his spot, and they exited the car. They headed over to the Longwood benches. Sean really wasn't feeling it. He was actually nervous as hell. Spank seen them approaching, and broke into a smile. Sean nervously smiled back. "Don't worry my nigga, shit is going to be alright." Spank said trying to encourage him.

"I don't know dawg. I got to find out what happened to them two niggas that I hit. I ain't trying to have no bodies."

"That shit is part of the game. You can't sign up for the game, and expect not to experience everything that comes along with it, you feel me?"

"I feel you, but damn this shit is crazy. I'm just trying to make a living."

"That may be true, but you're trying to do it in a dirty game. This ain't a 9 to 5 job. Niggas don't play by any rules in this shit. You got to get it together my nigga. What's done is done. We just got to make sure that you come out of this shit straight. Best believe after this, you ain't go have to worry about anyone else trying you. Now come over here, and get a beer."

They both walked over to where the coolers were at. Spank reached in and grabbed two Coronas, and handed one to Sean. He then called Tink over to fire up a blunt. Tink walked over and gave Sean a hug.

"We got you, we are family." he said to Sean. Sean started to feel a little better knowing that they had his back. He tried to relax and asked to hit the blunt.

"Fo sho!" Tink said and passed him the blunt. Spank draped his arm around him and said, "You been through enough drama for today, so you might want to get up out of here."

"Why, what's going on?"

"Me and that bitch Disco got into it out on the court, and he stole on me. After the game I'm going to tear this bitch up." Sean really did not want to be part of any more drama that day, but he knows that he has to stand by Spank no matter what.

"I'm with you, dawg. Whatever you be about, I be about."

"That's my nigga. I knew you would have my back." Spank responded.

Tink couldn't figure out why Spank was always quick to be on some bullshit. One could look at Tink's size and assume that he would be quick to get on some bullshit. In actuality Tink was the better thinker of the two, and often found him trying to reason with Spank. Tink wanted Sean to come down, to be around his people, but he didn't want him caught up in more shit than he already was in. Spank didn't have much of a conscience.

He preached about being a family, but at the end of the day, Spank was for himself. Rather he was wrong or right if he gets into something he expects those around him to ride with him no matter what the consequences may be. Spank was not going to let somebody like Disco humiliate him, in front of all these people that looked up to him and get away with it. He was going to whoop Disco as soon as this game was over with, or so he thought.

19

D-Nut and Crazy pulled up to a garage out in East Cleveland. They were driving back to back. D-Nut blew his horn, and the garage door rose. D-Nut pulled inside with Crazy following behind him. There were two more guys inside. Once they pulled all the way in the garage door closed. T-Smooth and Spaz walked over to the cars. D-Nut and Crazy each got out. Spaz said, "Damn where y'all came up on this at? This bitch tight!"

"We caught a crab slipping down by the Valley." D-Nut told him.

"Them project niggas slipping like that?"

Crazy jumped in "They bleed just like us. It ain't no rougher down there than it is out here."

"I know that's right" D-Nut chimed in.

The four of them belong to a Blood gang. D-Nut having been put on first by LA Dee, he recruited his three home boys. They all belong to the M.O.B set. The four of them specialized in car theft and carjacking. D-Nut spent a summer in Cali with Dee, and witnessed firsthand the art of carjacking. It fascinated him so much, that as soon as he got back home, he pulled one by himself. He then introduced it to the rest of his crew.

The four of them have truly adopted that LA mentality. There are various ways that other set members bring in money, but these four stick strictly with cars.

"It's some type of big event going on down there in the Valley." Crazy told them.

"What type of event?" asked T-Smooth.

"I don't know, but it's a lot of niggas riding real big down there."

"Look we can just leave this one here for now and shoot back down there, to see if we can catch some more niggas slipping." stated D-Nut.

Crazy jumped in, "We can at least come up with two more."

"Okay let's roll." said Spaz.

"Hold up let me grab my tech!" T-Smooth told them. He grabbed his tech, and then the four of them got in Crazy's car, and headed back down towards the Valley. Crazy jumped on the freeway. Spaz spoke, "We got an order for a 745 BMW, and it has to be between a 2005 and a 2008. Plus I got sales for three sets of 24's."

"So now we know what to be on the lookout for, let's get this money." stated Crazy.

T-Smooth fired up a blunt and Crazy told him to put in America's most wanted. He put it in, and put it on track four Straight Jacking. They smoked the blunt and bobbed their heads as they headed for the Valley.

☐

Disco had been helping Duck coach. The Valley was up by twelve, with two minutes left in the third quarter. Disco called for a time out. He told them, "Listen fellas, we can do this. I just need y'all to spread the floor more, and tighten up on defense. So let's get back out there and play ball."

☐

Coco pulled back up, to the courts. There was no place to park, so Coco pulled as close as she could to the car parked by the curb, and turned on the hazard lights. "This bitch is jumping! Look at all these people!" Renee said all excited.

"Look at them niggas on the court." Silvia chimed in.

"I'm about to call Tink and let him know I'm here," Coco told them as she pulled out her phone. She called Tink, and he answered, "What up?"

"It's me boo, I'm parked out in the street, because there is not anyplace to park."

"Alright, I'm about to walk out to the street, when you see me blow the horn." He then walked over to Spank and told him, "I'm about to go holla at Coco real quick, she is parked in the street."

"Make sure she got them guns, too."

"Nigga, I ain't got to make sure about nothing with my bitch. I know she got them."

"My bad player!" Spank said laughing. Tink walked out in the middle of the street. Coco seen him and blew the horn. He turned and jogged towards her truck. She pulled out so that he could get in.

Coco told him, "I missed you boo." He could tell that she was high.

"Girl are you high?"

"Yeah I'm high and horny!" she told him as she reached over and grabbed his dick.

"Girl you are tripping, the game is almost over with."

"I can't wait, I need some now. Just pull it out and let me sit on it." She pulled down his zipper. He helped her pull his dick out. Coco lifted up her skirt to her waist, and climbed on top of Tink's lap. Tink slid her panties to the side, and she lowered herself onto him. She was facing away from him, and put her hands on the dash board for support. Tink used his thumbs to spread her ass cheeks, and to control her movements.

Coco's pussy was so good that sometimes it was hard for him to control his self. He wanted her to go slow, so that he could enjoy it for a while. Coco started breathing hard. Her pussy was on fire. She started trying to bounce down harder on his dick, but Tink was using his hands to control her rhythm. He laid his head back on the head-rest, and stretched his legs all the way out. He saw how badly she really wanted it, so he removed his hands, letting her go wild. Coco started bucking, and gyrating her hips at a fast pace. She started talking, "Daddy that's it, let momma have that dick." Her talking encouraged Tink, and he started rising up to meet her thrust. He put his hands on her shoulders, pulling her down as he pushed his hips up. She said, "Oh God, that feels so good!"

"That's it, take this dick, take it." She started to tremble and pant.

"I'm cumming!" She slammed her body down hard on him. She was grinding her pussy on his dick. Tink started cumming also, and stretched his leg out so far that he caught a Charlie horse. A painful knot appeared in his thigh. He tried to tell Coco to stop, but she was in a zone trying to get another nut. He tried to shake the knot out, but his leg kept cramping. He hit the button on the side of the seat, sliding the seat back as far as it would go. Finally the knot started to recede, and he relaxed. Coco caught her breath, she opened her eyes and said, "Oh my God!" She scrambled off of Tink and tried to straighten herself up.

"What is wrong?" Tink asked her.

"They are watching us," she said pointing over to the sidewalk. Tink turned and peeped a man and woman holding hands watching them. Tink smiled and waved at them. The man gave him the thumbs up, while the lady blushed. The couple took off walking. Coco said, "Boy you're crazy."

"Shit, this was your crazy idea, don't get scared now."

"Do you want to smoke this blunt with me?"

"Yeah, fire it up," Tink replied and they sat in the truck and smoked. Renee and Silvia were standing by the court. Silvia said, "Girl look at them niggas, they can all get it."

"Bitch you nasty!"

"Hoe, don't hate me, hate the game."

"Whatever girl, I'm about to go see if Allen is over there with Spank, that's my baby."

"Bitch, he just be good dicking your ass, he ain't your baby."

"Hater!" Renee called her as she walked towards the benches.

☐

Crazy pulled onto the street and they saw all the cars lined up on both sides of the streets. Some were even parked on the sidewalk.

Spaz got hyped, "Look at all these pretty mother fuckers." He said. Crazy drove slowly down the street, allowing them to scope out all the cars. D-Nut yelled, "Look, there goes a 745 right there!" T-Smooth jumped in, "That bitch is bad, and we can get fifteen gees for that."

"This is what we are after then" said Crazy.

"Let's see if we can park somewhere to keep an eye on it." stated T-Smooth. Crazy continued to drive slowly down the street looking for a place to park. He didn't see anyplace to park, so he decided to just keep circling the block.

20

Longwood had tied the game, with less than a minute left to play. Longwood had the ball, and were advancing down the court. Once they got to the top of the key, they spread the floor. Their goal was to let the clock run down and get the last shot. The crowd was hyped. People from the Valley were screaming defense, and the people from Longwood were yelling take him to the hole. Pep had the ball at the top of the key. He tried to crossover and Jerry stole the ball and threw it down the court to Oscar. Oscar who was all by himself went up, and did a reverse dunk at the buzzer. The Valley won the game 98 to 96. The Valley went crazy. The players and the residents were happy. Big Dame was elated, because he had just won over ten grand. He went over to thank the players and the coaches.

Spank was heated, he blamed Pep for losing the game. He went over and started yelling, "You stupid mother fucker. You cost me ten grand. I should whoop your bitch ass!" The Longwood players were getting upset at how Spank was treating Pep. They felt that they played their hearts out, in a team effort. No one person is to blame, and Spank's ridicule of Pep didn't sit well with them.

Tink seen that the game was over, and told Coco he had to go and see what's up. When he got close to the bench area, he heard Spank going off. He instantly knew that they had lost. Once again he went over and tried to calm him down. "Come on dawg, it's just a game. Let's square up with Dame and get up out of here." Spank had intentions of squaring up with more than Dame, he planned on squaring off with Disco.

Spank headed over to his car, went in the trunk and grabbed the pouch that contained the money. He headed over to Dame. He was a sore loser and for a minute thought of telling Dame to chalk it. He didn't want to seem petty in front of everybody, so he quickly put that idea out of his mind.

Dame and Disco were enclosed in a circle of players. Spank pushed through the crowd, with Tink and everybody else on his heels. Dame reached out to shake his hand, but Spank just dropped the bag at his feet. He then turned to Disco, "Let's fight nigga!"

"Go on man, I ain't on that bullshit. Take the loss like a man."

"Bitch! Fight me like a man."

"I can't get nothing out of fighting you. You done lost your money, ain't nothing else to gain."

"Nigga I got more to lose. Dame bet them ten stacks back on your boy, I bet I beat his ass."

"You know what, I'm sick of your punk ass. Front me the money Dame, if I lose to this nigga I will pay you back."

"You know I got faith in you." Dame told him.

Spank truly did not think that Disco would stand up to him, but he accepted the challenge. Now Spank had to follow through.

"Where you want to do it at?" he asked.

"We can do it on the concrete nigga." Dame spoke up.

"I will handle this." He walked over and grabbed the mic.

"Everybody clear the court, back up off the court." Everyone started to clear the court. They were all trying to figure out what was going on. Dame told them, "We got a fight that is about to take place.

These two men are going to fight until either one of them is down for the count, or one taps out."

The crowd became excited. Several people were placing their own bets. It was mostly Longwood people that were betting against people from the Valley. Everybody was trying to find a good spot, to watch the action. Some were standing on the bleachers, others were standing on top of cars.

Disco and Spank made their way to the center of the court. They both removed their shirts, and put their hands up. Disco is a south paw, and Spank took note to stay on his right side as they approached each other. They were moving around in a circle, trying to feel each other out. Spank shot a jab, which Disco easily got out of the way of. Spank moved back in, and threw a left jab and a right hook. This time Disco did not move out of the way. He ducked the punches and came up with a right upper cut. The blow staggered Spank and caused him to bite his tongue. He backed up, to get his composure. Disco didn't even try to advance on him. He let Spank get his self back together.

"Nigga, you hit like a bitch!" Spank said. Disco just smiled and stayed focused. Spank tried another tactic. He faked a punch and rushed Disco. He wrapped his arms around his waist, trying to pick him up. This was the wrong move. Disco used his knee and kicked Spank in the chest, almost knocking the wind out of him. Spank released his hold, and tried to back up. Disco followed up this time, catching Spank with a straight right and a left hook, which put Spank on his ass. Tink rushed out on the court saying, "It's over! He wasn't going to keep watching his partner get humiliated. Disco turned and started to walk off the court, when Spank screamed at Tink, "Get off the court!" Then he yelled at disco, "It ain't over!" Tink just shook his head and walked off the court.

The Valley was yelling for Disco to finish him. The Longwood crew were ready to set it off. Disco turned and walked back towards Spank. Spank got up and brushed his self off. Disco told him, "I'm about to give you what you're looking for."

"Bring it on bitch!" Disco just smiled again and threw his hands up. This time Disco was the aggressor. He went at Spank hard throwing blows. Spank back peddled. "Don't run now!" Disco yelled. Spank started to lose confidence, and wanted to just shoot him. He knew that he needed to save face in front of his hood. He charged at Disco, and swung a hay maker. This move caught Disco off guard, and the blow grazed his chin. He knew that if he had gotten hit flush with that, he might have gone down for the count. He backed up and this gave Spank the impression that he was hurt. Spank lunged again throwing another wild hay maker, only this time Disco ducked. The wild swing took Spank off balance, almost causing him to turn in a circle.

When Disco rose up, he caught him with an upper cut and a left hook. Spank went down again, that time he went flat on his back. The Longwood crew couldn't believe it. Instead of paying their debt they started fighting. Tink, Allen and Sean rushed onto the court to help Spank.

Sikey wanted to prove to Spank that he is down with him so he began letting off shots. Disco got hit in the shoulder and went down. People from the Valley started shooting back. Tink took off towards Coco's truck to get the guns. Sean helped Spank to his feet and they took off running, crouching low. They were in the crossfire, and took cover behind the bleachers. Tink grabbed two guns out of Coco's truck and ran back to give them cover. He yelled for them to come on and started shooting.

Crazy and his crew saw all the commotion and the people fleeing.

Spaz said, "What the fuck is going on?"

"Shit it looks like they are having a shootout!" Crazy replied.

"Damn, this shit is going to fuck our lick up!" stated T-Smooth.

"This is even better I'm going to park at the end of the street and lay on him.

Allen joined the fire fight. The Valley started to retreat, getting fired on from different angles. Allen and Sean jumped in Allen's car, Tink jumped in the truck with Coco and Spank jumped in his BMW. Two of the cars pulled off. Allen was having trouble with his car. Coco made the light, but it caught Spank. When Spank stopped his car he was hit in the back. He looked in his rear view mirror and saw four occupants in the other car. Someone on the passenger's side was exiting the car. Spank instantly knew it was a jack move. He quickly jumped out of the car. D-nut approached him not knowing that there was a gun in his hand. As he came around the car, his eyes got big and he tried to raise the weapon that he had at his side. Before he could raise it, Spank hit him twice in the chest. Crazy said, "Holy shit!" and threw the car in reverse trying to back up. Spank let off shots hitting the car. Bullets crashed through the front window. T-Smooth was shooting from inside the car through the windshield. Crazy threw the car back in drive and pulled around the BMW. Spank dove on the side of his car, as bullets from the tech riddled his car.

Crazy turned the corner and headed back towards the freeway. Allen finally pulled up. Allen and Sean took in the scene and imagined the worst. Spank stood up, and the two of them became relieved. They yelled and told Spank to come on. He jumped back in his car, and they sped off leaving D-Nut lying dead in the street. The courts were in total chaos. Not only Disco got hit, but a little girl was also laid out by a stray bullet. People were screaming for someone to call the paramedics. Had Dame knew that the girl was shot, he would have put her in the car like he did with Disco. He rushed him to the hospital, while the little girl laid on the concrete bleeding to death.

21

Tee had the young dude park in front of Kayla's house. He called Kayla's phone and when she answered, he told her to open up the door. He gave the young boy the two hundred dollars, and exited the car when Kayla's front door opened. When Kayla saw his face she gasped. The blood and guns also frightened her. She ushered him into the house, and closed the door.

"Baby, what happened to you?"

"I had a little problem, and I need to lay low for a minute. Is it alright for me to chill here for a couple days?" Kayla debated with herself for a minute then she said, "I guess so, but don't you need to see somebody about your mouth?"

"My teeth are gone. It ain't like I need surgery. I will get them taken care of. Just get me some rags and let me go into the bathroom and clean myself up." Kayla went to the hall closet, and grabbed some towels. She started second guessing herself, hoping that she doesn't have to face any consequences behind her decision to let him stay there.

□

The little girl was loaded into the ambulance. Her mother was riding with her, praying that her daughter pulls through. She did not think that attending a basketball game could turn out so violently. Her daughter got hit in the stomach and had internal bleeding but her pulse and heartbeat were good. Homicide was down in the Valley, trying to put together what took place. So far they have found out that a basketball game had taken place between Longwood and Garden Valley and that it turned violent. They are trying to figure out what side is the dead man lying in the street from. None of the witnesses seem to recognize him. It was odd to the detectives, that the guy had one red bandana tied around his wrist and another one hanging out of his back right pocket.

Detective Jenkins said to his partner, "It's been a very busy day."

"Yeah, I wonder what's so special about it."

"Well, it looks like this might be overtime for the next couple of months."

"If they keep the killings up at this rate, we are going 24 hour shifts."

"If we do that after a while we will find ourselves lying on a slab beside one of them."

"Well, we might as well call it a night. The Captain has requested to see us in the morning. We might as well get our last good night of sleep."

They got in their car and headed for the district. Detective Jenkins is a black, 45-year old homicide detective. He has been married and divorced twice, with two kids. His marriages failed, because his ex-wives felt that he was married to his job. He started out as a foot patrol officer. He was so dedicated to his job that he quickly rose up through the ranks. Now he is considered one of the best homicide detectives in his district. Becoming detective was a big accomplishment for him, being that he grew up in the projects to a single mother, in one of the roughest projects in Cleveland. He does not believe in excuses as to why people commit crimes. To him it's all about choices, and he made the right ones, by joining the military and the police force.

His partner is Detective Howard. A white, 45- yearold married man. He is a third generation police officer, and is a hard nose. When he was a patrolman he had numerous complaints lodged against him for use of excessive force, still he made detective. He currently has a son in the police academy. He never interacted with blacks on a business or personal level until he became a police officer. He and Detective Jenkins have been partners for two years now. They are friends outside of work.

His relationship with Jenkins has helped him to break the stereotype that he had placed on all black people. Together they are like the dynamic duo, when it comes to solving murders and violent crimes. Being called in by the captain, they knew that the heat was about to be on.

22

Tink, Spank, Allen and Sean all were down in a parking lot in Longwood.

"I told you to just let that shit go. It wasn't worth it!" Tink told him.

"Nigga, I ain't the one that started shooting."

"Yeah but you knew that them young niggas were going to act a fool about you. We better hope that no one got hurt."

"Well I almost got carjacked and had to lay a nigga down."

"You almost got carjacked, when?"

"When we were leaving and I got caught at the light."

"Damn man! We might have to leave town and lay low for a little bit. Look I'm going to send Coco back up there to see what's up."

"Yeah do that, I'm about to go and stash my car. Sean what you going to do? If we jet, are you going with us?"

"Naw Spank! I got to take care of business. I'm going to just lay low at my girl's house. Somebody has got to stay here and handle business."

"That's what's up. We will check in with you to see what is going on. Allen shoot him to where he has to go."

Tink sent Coco back up to the Valley to get the scoop on how many people got hurt. She found out that an innocent little girl got shot, Disco got shot and that a man died on the corner. She also found out that homicide knows that Longwood is involved. Tink told her to pack some bags because they are going to Florida. Spank doesn't agree with his decision to take Coco along. Why take sand to the beach. He plans on going down there as a single man.

☐

Man called and hooked up with Linda. They have been fucking off and on for over three years. They were up in a hotel. They had just got through sexing, when Man put his plan in motion.

"L, I need you to do me a favor. I need some information and I need you to be discreet about it."

"What is it?"

"Sean, that dude that roll with your girl Coco's dude. I need to know where he lay his head at. I know Coco your girl, but this some personal shit."

"Fuck Coco! We ain't like that. I'll try to do that for you but just make sure my name don't pop up."

"I got you, baby girl. I owe you one."

"Nigga, you owe me two."

"Okay you got that." Linda was mad at Coco, and out of revenge was willing to sell Sean out. She had to figure out how she could get an address for where Sean stayed. She figured her first shot would be with Silvia.

☐

Sean had Allen drop him off out in Indian hills, at his girl Meka's house. He kept Meka a secret, and nobody knew that she was his main girl and that this is where he truly laid his head. He had no other option, that's why he allowed Allen to bring him out there. Meka is mixed with Asian and black. She is a sales rep for an insurance company. Sean had plans of one day getting out of the game and settling down with her, now he doesn't know what the future holds. He didn't tell her anything and tried to act normal even though he was really scared.

Tink, Coco and Spank boarded a plane headed for Florida. They left Allen behind, who was supposed to be the go between for them and Sean. He also had to watch over the workers. To Spank it was about to be fun in the sun.

23

Detectives Jenkins and Howard were in Captain Smith's office, knowing that trouble was brewing.

"Gentlemen it's plain and simple. Its election time and the Mayor is running for re-election. He is all up in my ass about this violent spree that seems to be going on throughout the city. If the city doesn't feel safe, they are going to feel that he isn't doing his job. If he loses, then I lose. If I lose then you lose, you get it?" They both nodded their heads.

"Jenkins fill me in on what you have so far."

"Well Cap, concerning the shooting in Morris Black, there are two witnesses that we have yet to question due to medical reasons."

"So the only witnesses that you have are in the hospital?"

"Yes sir."

"What about the First Merit robbery and homicide?"

"Well we have one suspect in custody, and we are still looking for the shooter."

"I heard that a little girl was shot in the Garden Valley shooting and a man was left dead in the middle of the street. What's the update on that situation?"

"The little girl was hit by a stray bullet. Two different neighborhoods were playing basketball against each other when they got into a confrontation. It escalated to a shooting. The guy that was found in the middle of the street we haven't connected him with either one of the neighborhoods."

"How is the little girl?"

"She was shot in the stomach. She had surgery and was fitted with a colostomy bag."

"Useless thugs can be understood, but innocent little kids cannot be accepted. Listen you two have a week to wrap these cases up. We got to show the public that we act swiftly when it comes to violence. The citizens want to feel safe and it's your job to make it happen. Now get out there and get some results." Jenkins and Howard headed out of the captain's office.

"So where do we start?" Howard asked.

"Well, the kid that was involved in the robbery only has a broken leg, so we can start with questioning him. Also I ran the plates off the car and they came back to a Tiffany Porter, with an address listed as 2931 East 121st. So that will be our second stop if the kid doesn't cooperate."

"Okay I'll drive." Jenkins throws him the car keys as they approached the vehicle.

Derrick was cuffed to a bed at Charity hospital. There was a police officer posted outside his door. He is awake and tried to use the phone, but the line was dead. He is still in pain, from his leg and his spleen being repaired.

Two detectives walked into his room, and introduced themselves. They asked him if they could ask him a few questions to which he agreed. Jenkins first read him his rights, and then started in with the questioning.

"Where is your friend?"

"What friend?"

"Don't play stupid, the friend that you robbed the bank with."

"I didn't rob no bank. I was just getting a ride."

"Do you expect us to believe that you were just getting a ride and that the driver just happened to stop and rob a bank without you knowing it?"

"I don't care what you believe, but that's the truth."

"Alright let me be straight with you Mr. Wright, the security guard that was shot died, and right now you're the only one that we have in custody. Now if you want to take the fall all by yourself, be my guest."

"I ain't taking no fall, because I didn't do shit!"

Detective Howard jumped in, "Look okay just give us the name of the person that was giving you a ride."

"I just know him by Tee."

"Do you know where this Tee lives or hangs out?"

"No I don't."

"Well how did he end up giving you a ride?"

"Look I'm through talking, I want a lawyer."

"If you are innocent as you say, then you don't need a lawyer, but have it your way. You can call him, once you get booked into the county jail. You have a nice day, and if you find that you want to talk here is my card." Detectives Jenkins and Howard left Derrick's room.

"What do we do next?" asked Howard.

"We go and talk to Ms. Porter." They headed out the hospital to their car.

24

Tink, Coco and Spank landed in Miami and checked in to a Ritz Carlton hotel. They got adjoining rooms. Tink and Coco decided to stay in the room the first night. Spank went straight down to the bar, in search of a nice lady. Being as it was an upscale hotel, he did not really see any one to his liking. He likes hood chicks. He stepped outside and asked a valet where the best strip club was. After the valet informed him of the location, he had the valet hail him a cab. He was going to rent a car the next day, but for now he needed transportation.

Spank pulled up to Diamond's strip club, he paid the fare and exited the cab. Spank fit right in. He was dressed like a baller, and was wearing some of his best jewelry. He got a front table, and ordered a bottle of Cristal. He was amazed at how beautiful the girls were. Most of them were of mixed descent. He was throwing mass money to the dancers on stage. A dancer approached him and introduced herself, "Hi I'm Cherry, would you like a lap dance?" Spank looked her up and down and could not believe his eyes. She was the most beautiful woman that he had ever seen. She looked like she was pure Indian, with long black silky hair that flowed down her back. The thong let her bronze beautiful ass hang out. Spank told her, "Yeah I will have one, then again with you I may take two." Cherry just smiled, and started to dance to Mystical's *Shake It Fast*. Spank just sat hypnotized by her exotic appearance. She straddled him, facing away and bent over. Her pussy lips hung out of her thong. I got to have this, Spank said to his self. Even though he did not trick, he was willing to spend whatever it took to take her back to the hotel. After the dance was over Cherry started to walk away, but Spank grabbed her hand.

He asked her, "Where are you going?"

"I'm working, I have to go make some more money."

"Look, I'm going to pay you for another lap dance, but I just want to talk to you, is that cool?"

"As long as you know that I'm on the clock, so when the song stops I'm gone."

"I might as well wait for a new song to start then."

"I like you, I will give you two songs. What do you want to talk about?"

"First, do you have a man?"

"No, I do not have a man."

"Do you date outside of the club?"

"It depends, but look I ain't no hoe."

"I wasn't trying to imply that you were. It's just that I am visiting from out of town, and would like to have you show me around. I would like to get to know you."

"How long will you be here?"

"At least a couple of weeks. I don't want to be alone. We could have fun, if you give it a try."

"It's something about you. You are very charismatic. I'm going to give you my number. You call me and we will go from there."

"That's all I ask for ma, is an opportunity. You won't regret it."

"I hope not," she told him as she smiled and walked away. Spank was ready to leave. He stepped outside to hail a cab.

□

Back in Cleveland, Allen was making rounds, and collecting money from the workers. He was to meet with Sean in the morning to give him the money and pick up more dope. It was about ten at night when he got through making his rounds. He thought he would shoot down to Jack's bar and have a few drinks, and meet Sean in the morning. It was Wednesday night, one of the nights that Jack's be jumping. Three neighborhoods usually went to Jack's bar, down the way, the Valley and the Cedar neighborhood. Jack's is a small bar, with only one way in and one way out. The bouncers showed favoritism, by letting some guys enter with their guns. Jack's was always prone to violence. Allen entered the bar and was shoulder to shoulder with people. His cellphone vibrated on his hip. He looked and seen that it was Sean calling. He answered it, "What's up my nigga?"

"I need those ends, because I got to re-up in the morning."

"I got the money with me, but I'm down here at Jack's. You can shoot down here and get it and have a drink with me."

"I don't know about any drinks, but I'm coming to get that money. I'll call you when I get outside."

"Bet my nigga!" Allen said and hung up the phone. Sean has been real low key. Only coming out at night, using his girl's car. He still hasn't heard anything about his name being linked to any shooting, but he was still being cautious trying to stay under the radar.

Linda was up in Jack's that night. She was sitting at the bar nursing a drink. She had tried to get information from Silvia on where Sean laid his head at, by telling her that she was trying to get with him. Silvia could not provide her with any information. So she sat wondering what her next move would be. Someone approached her and offered to buy her another drink, which she gladly accepted.

He sat on the seat next to hers and introduced his self. He was having a one way conversation with her since her mind was somewhere else. She really liked Man and wanted to prove to him that she was down.

Allen was sitting at the bar, when Nanky approached him, "Allen, right?"

"Yeah what's up Nanky?"

"You still remember my name, huh?"

"I never forget a pretty girl's name."

"Well can you buy a pretty girl a drink?"

"No problem, what are you drinking?"

"Grey Goose."

"Bartender, give the lady a double of Goose." Allen wanted to fuck Nanky since Spud was fucking with Spank. He thought this might be his lucky night.

"Thanks, so who are you here with?" Nanky asked him.

"I'm here by myself, just having a few drinks before I call it a night. Who are you here with?"

"I came with a couple of my girlfriends, but they have plans once they leave here."

"So what are you trying to get into?"

"I just want to have a few drinks and chill."

"I'm waiting to meet somebody, after they come we can go and get something to eat and see where the night leads us."

"That's cool, just let me go and tell my girls that I'm going to roll with you."

"I will be right here." Nanky went in search of Spud and Robbin to tell them that she had a lick lined up. She knew that Allen was down with Spank and Tink, and thought that he was rolling. She figured that she could get him to take her to a hotel, fuck him until he passes out, then she could roll his pockets and get his jewelry. She found her girls and told them that she had a lick and would call them to come and get her later. Had she mentioned that the lick was Allen, Spud would have warned her about how dangerous he was. Nanky joined Allen back at the bar.

Sean pulled up outside of Jack's and called Allen's phone, "Al, I'm outside."

"Sean park and come in. Have one drink, I'm buying."

"I'm kind of in a hurry."

"Come on man, one drink."

"Okay, one drink. Let me find a place to park." It was super crowded. As he made his way through the crowd Linda spotted him. She left the guy that was talking to her, sitting at the bar by himself. She said as she approached Sean, "Hey Sean." He turned around and was surprised to see Linda. He knew that Linda was Coco's friend. She was alright in the face, but had a bad ass body. He always wanted to fuck her.

"What's up Linda?"

"Nothing, up here bored."

"I ain't staying long, I'm just here to meet somebody right quick, and then I got to roll out."

"Take my number and call me. Coco went out of town and I have nothing to do, we can kick it."

"Okay let me put your number in my phone." Linda gave him her number and he took off in search of Allen.

Linda pulled out her phone and called Man. He answered. "Who dis?"

"Man, it's Linda, you got to get down here to Jack's fast. Sean is down here."

Man got hyped, "Shit, try to keep him there. I'm on my way!"

"You got to hurry up, he said he is only here to meet somebody, and then he is gone."

"Okay just try to stall him, I'm on my way." He hung up from her and called Jerrel's phone and it went straight to voice mail. He hung up and tried it again. After getting the same results, he left a message telling Jerrel to get Ray Ray and Tez and meet him down at Jack's. He grabbed his pistol, jumped in his car and headed for Jack's.

Sean approached Allen at the bar. He recognized Nanky sitting with him.

"What are you drinking?" Allen asked him.

"Just give me a double Jack and coke."

"Bartender give this man a double Jack and coke."

"Have you heard from Spank or Tink yet?" Sean asked.

"Yeah Spank hollered at me when they touched down. He said after they got settled in that he would holla back at me. What's been up with you?"

"I just been chilling."

"Do you need me to do anything?"

"Yeah, I might need you to shoot up to Saint Luke's to see how old girl is doing and to let her know that I haven't forgotten about her."

"I can do that for you, just let me know when."

"Bet," Sean said as he downed his drink.

"Peep I need to get that bread so I can roll."

"For sure, come on baby girl we about to blow this spot." Allen, Nanky and Sean were heading out of the bar, when Linda approached Sean, "So why are you about to leave so quickly? Keep me company for a little bit."

"I would love to get with you, but I'm on a mission right now. I'm definitely going to get at you within the next couple of days."

"Okay you do that." Linda was frustrated, but knew that there wasn't anything that she could do.

Allen led the way to his car. He opened the trunk and gave Sean the money. Sean told him to follow him to his car so that he could give him the dope. Allen let Nanky sit in his car while they conducted the transactions. Nanky was very observant, and seen Allen go into his trunk twice. Jackpot, she thought to herself. Allen got in the car and asked her, "Are you in the mood foe some Chinese food?"

"I could go for some shrimp fried rice, with some duck sauce."

"There it is then, we are on our way to the Chinese spot."

By the time Man got down to Jack's, Sean was long gone. Linda was standing outside, and when he walked up she said, "It's too late."

"Damn, you couldn't stall him?"

"The nigga was in a hurry. He said he was on a mission."

"Fuck! We probably won't get another chance."

"Calm down, he been wanting to fuck me for a while now. He took my number and said that he would be calling me within a couple of days."

"That's cool, it will give me a chance to get my people together. I'll get up with you."

"Nigga fuck that, take me with you. I don't want to be by myself tonight."

"Shit, we are going to have to get a room."

"That's fine by me, long as you put it on me." They got in his car and he drove towards Crosstown Motel.

25

Allen took Nanky to a Chinese spot once they were given their orders, they got back in the car and headed for a motel. Allen did not think that she was worthy of a hotel, so he took her to the Western Inn. Once they were in the room Allen wasted no time stripping down to his boxers.

"You move quickly don't you?" Nanky said.

"Ain't no sense in beating around the bush. You need to come up out of those clothes."

Nanky sat her food down on the dresser. She knew that she would have to put it on him, to knock him out. She started taking her clothes off. By the time she was down to her panties and bra, Allen was rock hard. She had a beautiful body. Her titties sat up high, she had a small waist, and a fat ass that had no blemishes.

Allen stood up and stripped out of his boxers. Nanky looked down and hesitated for a minute. She could not believe that his dick was that big. She wondered if she could handle it. Allen saw her hesitation and told her, "Don't worry baby girl, I'll be gentle with you." Nanky gave a nervous smile, and continued to undress. Allen motioned for her to come over to the bed. He sat down and had her stand in front of him. He took his hand and put it between her legs. She opened them wider, and he stuck two fingers in her. She was super wet. He pulled his fingers out, and put them up to his nose. After liking the smell, he put the fingers into his mouth and sucked the juice off of them. He told her, "I got to suck this pussy." He stood up, got behind her and bent her over the bed. He then got down on his knees, spread her ass cheeks and started eating her from the back. Nanky couldn't believe what he was doing. He is a freaky mother fucker, she thought to herself.

Nanky began to moan as her body reacted to what he was doing to her. She could not control her body. Her pussy was leaking fluids all over his mouth. Suddenly, Allen stood up and had her sit on the bed. He stood in front of her and put his dick to her mouth. She opened her mouth wide and he stuck his dick in her mouth. She could only get one fourth of his dick in her mouth. She put two hands on it and commenced to sucking and licking on it. Allen put both of his hands on the side of her head to hold it still then he started fucking her in the mouth. Nanky had her eyes closed making slurping sounds. The feeling was getting too good for Allen to handle, so he stopped her. He had her stand back up, and bend over on the bed. He spit on two of us fingers and put them down to her pussy to give it an extra moistening. Then he spit on the head of his dick. He knew that even though she was super wet, that it still was going to be a hard fit.

He put his dick inside her pussy, and instantly felt resistance. He rubbed the head up and down the slit, while trying to force it in. When the head penetrated the opening, Nanky gasped. She felt like she was already full. She braced her hands on the bed for support. Allen kept sinking deeper and deeper. Once he was half way in, he started to go in and out of her. Nanky told him, "Take it slow please, your dick is too big."

"Don't worry ma you're a big girl, you can take it." He picked his rhythm up. The pain started turning into pleasure for Nanky, and she started fucking him back. Allen was ball deep in her. Her ass cheeks shook every time he slammed against them. Nanky was on the verge of climaxing.

"Right there daddy, right there."

"That's it baby girl take this dick" he told her as he relentlessly pounded her. All of a sudden she started to shudder and fell onto the bed, with him falling right along with her. Her arms were stretched out, and he had his fingers interlocked with hers as he continued to pound her. He felt the heat rise in his balls and knew that he was about to cum. He slammed into her one last time, and then just laid on top of her shooting his sperm in her. When he was done he rolled off of her onto his back. They both laid there still for a minute trying to catch their breathe. Once Nanky caught her breathe she turned to him and said, "Damn I should have gotten with you a long time ago!" She had never been fucked like that before. She still had a job to do, so she curled up to him and waited for him to fall asleep. After about thirty minutes his breathing became labored. It seemed like he was sleeping peacefully. Nanky quietly got up and put her clothes on. She grabbed his pants and went into the bathroom. She closed the door and called Spud as she went through his pockets. Spud answered and she told her to come pick her up from the motel. She took everything out of his pockets and tucked his car keys in her pocket. She left out of the bathroom and headed for the door. She was almost to the door, When Allen's voice startled her, "Where are you going?" Nervously she told him that she was only going to the lobby to get something to drink. "Okay hurry back," he said as he rolled over.

She quickly left out of the room. Allen thought for a second, and then he got up and reached for his pants which were no longer next to the bed. He hurried up and threw on his boxers and ran out of the room. As he was headed for his car, he seen that his trunk was open. "I'm going to kill this bitch!" Allen said to himself.

Nanky was bent over rambling through his trunk, so she didn't hear when he approached her. Allen grabbed her by her hair, and snatched her up so hard that her head hit the trunk.

"Bitch you trying to rob me?"

"No, please I'm sorry."

"Sorry didn't do it bitch! You did!" he yelled as he started dragging her back towards the hotel room. Nanky started screaming, and he put one of his hands over her mouth as he continued to drag her. Nanky was kicking and trying to bite his hand. She thought he might kill her. Allen got her in the room and closed the door.

"You want to try to steal from me? You thought you were slick? I should kill you bitch."

"Please I'm sorry, I'll make it up to you."

"Yeah you go make it up to me alright!" he told her as he started punching her in the face. The one thing Allen hated was for someone to try and play him like a sucker. He beat Nanky until she was unconscious, then he hurried up and put on his clothes, he grabbed his car keys and jetted. He was glad that he had put the room in an alias name.

In Miami Spank went and rented a 2007 Dodge Magnum, and Tink rented a Charger. He and Coco decided to go shopping while Spank called Cherry and took her to lunch. Spank found out that she was stripping to pay her college tuition to get her major in Psychology. He also found out that she was 24 years old with no kids. As it turned out, the name Cherry was short for Cherokee, which was her heritage.

After lunch Cherry gave him directions on a tour of the city. Spank wanted to spend the whole day with her, but she told him that she needed to get home to get ready for work.

"Do you like your job?" Spank asked her.

"It pays the bills, that's all that matters."

"So, when can I see you again?"

'Tell you what, I don't have to work tomorrow night. We can spend the whole day together. But we are going to have to do the things that I want to do."

"Okay, that's a bet." He dropped her off and headed back to his hotel room. When he got back to the room, he went to go and holla at Tink. As he approached the door he heard loud moans. He cracked the door and saw that Tink was banging Coco doggy style. They were facing away from him. There was a mirror at the head of the bed. Tink had his eyes closed, and Coco's head was down. He opened the door a little further, when all of a sudden Coco opened her eyes. Looking in the mirror she could see Spank. They locked eyes for a moment, and then she dropped her head back down and continued to moan. Spank slowly closed the door, went and turned the TV on and flopped down on the bed.

☐

Back in Cleveland Detective Jenkins and Howard arrived at Tiffany Porter's address. It was a small house in a nice neighborhood. Jenkins knocked on the door.

"Who is it?" a voice asked.

"This is Detective Jenkins from the Cleveland police department. I am looking for a Ms. Tiffany Porter." She opened the door.

"Yes, I am her."

"We would like to ask you some questions concerning a 2003 Regal that is registered to your name."

"What about it?"

"Do you still have that car ma'am?"

"No, I sold that car a year ago."

"Who did you sell it to?"

"Some man seen it sitting outside, with the For Sale sign in the window, and came and bought it."

"Then why is the car still registered in your name?"

"He bought it on a weekend and was supposed to return the following Monday so that we could switch the paperwork over, but he never came back."

"And you don't know his name?"

"No, I don't."

"Ms. Porter it's kind of hard for us to believe, that you sold your car to a person that you did not know, without switching the car out of your name or removing the plates."

"Well, that's what happened. What is this about anyway?"

"Your car was used in a bank robbery in which a security guard was killed. The car was impounded and is being dusted for prints, and if through our investigation we later find out that you lied to us, you will be charged with hindering a police investigation. You could possibly be charged with complicity to aggravated murder."

"Do you understand?" asked Detective Jenkins.

"Look, I got kids and a job that I need to keep. The car belongs to my cousin. He did not have any driver's license, so I let him put it in my name."

"And what is your cousin's name?"

"Tavon Williams."

"Do you have an address for him, or an address that he's known to frequent?"

"No, but he frequently hangs out in the Garden Valley projects."

"Ms. Porter we appreciate your time, and if you happen to come across any more information that could lead us to Mr. Williams, please call us at this number." Jenkins handed her his card and they left her residence.

Jenkins told Howard to call Tavon Williams in and see what comes back and if there is an address listed for him. He told him to also put out an APB on him, with an armed and dangerous warning.

☐

Derrick was transported to the county jail and booked, for aggravated robbery and aggravated murder with violent specifications. He called Stacey collect and she accepted, "Boy, where are you at?"

"I'm down at the County."

"For what?"

"Tee robbed a bank."

"What has that got to do with you?"

"I was in the car, but I didn't know he was going to do that."

"Nigga! I told your hard headed ass. So what are you calling me for?"

"Stacey don't play, they got me charged with murder."

"What! Why you charged?"

"Because Tee got away. I broke my legs when he crashed the car."

"So you tell them Tee's name, and they are going to let you go, right?"

"Stacey you know I can't do that I can't snitch."

"Nigga, you crazy, you say you didn't have shit to do with it, and he left you. So? Are you going to take the fall for it?"

"I ain't taking no fall, and I ain't snitching. Look I got a bond hearing in the morning, can you come?"

"Boy, you know I got to work, but I'm going to see. If I can't make it to your bond hearing, I will be down to visit you once I get off of work."

"Alright that's cool."

"Do you want me to call your mother and father?"

"No, let me think things out first."

"Okay I will see you tomorrow."

"I love you Stacey. I'm sorry that I didn't listen to you."

"Save that shit boy, I will be down there tomorrow." she told him then hung up.

Stacey was mad as hell at Derrick, but she did care for him and was not going to leave him for dead. She could not understand why he would keep quiet, and take the fall for a nigga that didn't give a fuck about him. She thought that Derrick was too naive to be in the streets. She would stick by him as best she could, but if he goes down for murder she will eventually have to move on with her life.

Derrick sat in the County on the medical floor. He was thinking of all the things that he could have done with his life. Maybe he should have joined the service like his father had suggested. He knew that Tee was crazy, but he did not think that he would rob a bank or kill someone. He certainly didn't think he'd leave him to take the blame. Maybe he could reach out to Tee through the streets to clear his name he thought to himself.

26

Fred had been staying at Shannon's house. The police had yet to locate his car. The insurance company was not going to settle the claim until the car was recovered.

Shannon had to take him to pick up some more clothes. On the way back he had her stop at Dailey's so that he could get some jerk chicken. As he was leaving the restaurant, Ronald and Doc were entering.

"Nigga where you been" asked Ronald.

"Nigga fuck you!"

"Man, you still tripping about that shit in the Valley" asked Doc.

"You niggas left me for dead. Right after y'all jumped out of my shit, I got shot and carjacked."

"And you blame us?" asked Ronald.

"You damn right, you niggas were so thirsty for some bitches that y'all left me hanging, when y'all should of had my back."

"Shit we're sorry, we ain't know that no shit like that was going to happen."

"It's all good, I'll holla at you niggas." Fred told them as he got back in the car.

☐

Nena was moved from recovery to a regular room. It hurt her to take deep breaths, but otherwise she was doing fine. The tubes had been removed from her throat, and she was given a machine that she was required to blow into three times every hour. It was used to keep fluid from building up in her lungs.

She remembered everything that happened vividly. She hoped that Sean was alright. She wasn't surprised that no one came to visit her. All of her family were back in New York. She did wonder why her friend Tammy had not been up there. So she reached over, picked up the phone and called her.

Tammy picked up, "Hello?"

"Bitch, why you ain't been up here to see me?"

"Where the fuck you at? I thought you were either still with that nigga or that you went back on the road."

"Girl how was I going to go on the road when all my stuff is at your house?"

"Girl that don't matter with you. Anyway why are you in there?"

"I got shot, I'm sitting up in Saint Luke's hospital. They say I could have died."

"You're lying girl, what room are you in? I'm about to come up there"

"I'm in room 314 on the third floor."

"Okay I'm on my way." Tammy told her and hung up. She knew Nena was crazy, but wondered how in the hell did she get shot. She felt Nena needed to slow down, maybe take a break for a while and decided she would tell her those things when she got to the hospital.

☐

Early the next morning Derrick was taken before a judge. He was assigned a public defender and his bond was set at $500,000. Stacey did not make the hearing, and he was transported back to the county. He knew that Stacey did not have that type of money, not even ten percent of it. It was time to call his parents, and let them know what was going on. They were going to be very upset, but he was their only son. There was no way that they were going to turn their backs on him.

He called collect, and his mother answered. She accepted the call, "What are you doing calling here collect? Where are you at?"

"I'm down town in the County ma."

"Hell no! What did you do?"

"Nothing ma, It's a big mistake."

"Okay a mistake, boy you better get your life together." His father heard his mother talking in a raised voice and asked her who she was talking to.

"It's your son, and you're not going to believe where he is calling from." His father picked up the kitchen phone.

"What's going on with you, Derrick?"

"Pops, they got me locked up for something that I didn't do."

"So what you're saying is that someone framed you?"

"No pops, I was with somebody that did something without my knowledge and they charged me with it."

"Boy, I told you that running around with them no good thugs out in them streets was going to be the death of you."

"I know pops. I need your help. They got me in a very bad situation."

"Well, what do you need? I ain't got much."

"I need you to get me a lawyer, and get me out on bond so that I can prove that I am innocent."

"And how much is your bond?"

"Its $500,000,"

"Boy is you crazy! I don't have that type of money."

"That's why I said get me a lawyer, because he can get my bond dropped and you can put the house up."

"Derrick you got some nerve, to call asking for us to sacrifice everything that we have worked hard for, when you refused to do any of the things that we asked of you. You know I love you son, but you're asking for a lot. I'm going to have to discuss this with your mother. Once we have made a decision I will let you know."

"So when can I call back?"

"We will decide something by tomorrow."

"Okay, I'll call back tomorrow."

"Derrick, get a bible and pray, you hear me?"

"Yeah, I hear you, pops." Derrick hung up the phone. Realization started to set in. He knew that he had really messed up. He swore that if he got out of this mess that he was going to get his life together. He went in search of a bible.

Derrick was a junior, he was his father's only son. His father was hurt by the trouble that his son had got caught up in. Him and his wife talked and came to the conclusion that he should be given a chance, and they agreed to help Derrick. They retained a lawyer, and sent him down to talk to him.

☐

Disco got released from the hospital with a fractured shoulder leaving his arm in a sling.

"Is you alright dawg?"

"Yeah I'm good, just got a little pain in my shoulder. They gave me some Tylenol with Codeine so I guess I will be good."

"That was some sucker shit. You know Pam's daughter Keisha got shot?"

"Get the fuck out of here!"

"I'm serious, she got hit in the stomach, and they had to put a shit bag on her."

"Damn, she's only eleven years old. We need to see them niggas for real Dame."

"Shit is too hot right now. Homicide has been down there sweating niggas."

"Why homicide?"

"Shit you ain't know, they found a nigga lying dead in the street at the corner of 73rd."

"Who was he?"

"That's the crazy part, he ain't from the Valley or Longwood."

"Yeah that's crazy."

"So we got to lay low. I am going over to Pam's house later on, to let her know that if she needs anything I got her."

"You a real nigga, man."

"I try to be in this unreal world."

"If you hungry? I could go for a nice juicy steak."
"Let's go down to the Best Steak and Gyro house."
"That's cool." Dame headed towards downtown.

27

Sean called Allen, "Al, what's up?"

"Not much, but you ain't go believe what happened. That bitch Nanky tried to rob me."

"How she do that?"

"I took her to a motel, and fucked her. When she thought I was sleep she rolled my pockets and took my car keys. I caught the bitch in my trunk."

"That bitch tried you like that?"

"Sean, I left that bitch unconscious in that room. These hoes are getting bold nowadays, what's good though?"

"I wanted to know if you could shoot up there and holla at old girl for me, and let her know that I haven't forgotten about her."

"What's her name again?"

"It's Nena Miles."

"I got you, when I get up there I'm going to call your phone and let you holla at her yourself."

"Okay, that's a bet."

"Alright I will hit you when I get up there." He grabbed his car keys and headed out the door.

Tammy got up to Saint Luke's and caught the elevator up to the third floor. She walked down the hall until she came to room 314.

As she entered the room she saw tubes and wires attached to Nena, and she wanted to cry. Nena looked up and gave a weak smile, "Hey girl."

"Damn Nena look at you, what happened boo?"

"I was with Sean, when these guys tried to rob him."

"So, where is he at?"

"I don't know, but I guess he was the one that brought me here."

"Just dropped you off and left huh?"

"Girl he probably didn't want to get questioned by the police. Plus he had dope on him."

"Girl you need to slow your roll, fall back. Go back to school or something, but get out of these streets."

"Yeah, I feel you girl. They had to fix my lung, so I won't be able to dance for a minute. My doctor said that I can probably be released Monday. You know that they are going to rush me out, because I don't have any insurance."

"Well you can stay with me, until you heal up and decide what you are going to do."

"Thanks girl, I really appreciate it."

"That's what friends are for."

Allen walked in the room and shocked them both. Nena became apprehensive.

"What are you doing in here?" she asked him as she went towards the phone.

Allen smiled, "Chill baby sis I came out of love. My dawg Sean sent me up here to check on his lady." That comment did not go unnoticed by Nena, and she perked up, "Where is he?" she asked excitedly.

"Hold on I'm going to call him for you right now." He called Sean's phone, and he answered, "Yo Sean I'm here with your lady she wants to speak to you," he handed her the phone.

Sean asked her, "How are you doing?"

"I'm fine, just ready to get up out of here."

"Look I'm sorry you got caught up in that mess. I knew that I shouldn't have mixed business with pleasure."

"I'm a big girl Sean, shit happens. I'm just glad that you are alright and that you didn't forget about me."

"Never that, baby girl. I just been laying low, because I don't know what the word is out in them streets. When things blow over I will be up there to see you okay?"

"Yeah, okay."

"So have the police been to see you yet?"

"Nope, nobody been up here. But don't worry I got you."

"That's what's up. If you need anything do not hesitate to ask. Let me holla back at Al."

"Shit he over there sweating my girl, hold on." She called Allen and gave him the phone, "Thanks my nigga." Sean told him.

"It's all love fam, plus I just came up. I'm about to bounce with her friend."

"Pimp nigga, pimp." Sean told him then hung up. Tammy told Nena that Allen was giving her a ride home and that she would be back to see her the next day.

Derrick was called for a visit. He was taken down to the sixth floor, and was led into a room that was lined with visiting booths. The visits were conducted through glass. Stacey was already sitting down when he entered. He picked up the receiver, "What's good?"

"Shit, ain't nothing good. Your ass is in here and I had to find a way down here to see you."

"Well I might be out soon."

"And how do you figure that?"

"I talked to my pops and he might hire me a lawyer and put up the house to get me out on bond."

"You still are going to have the charges. Why don't you just tell the people the truth Derrick? This is crazy, that nigga don't give a damn about you."

"It's the principal Stace. When I get out I'm going to clear my name, I just got to find Tee."

"Nigga, you are living in a fantasy world, this shit ain't TV. These people are going to give you life."

"I ain't about to argue Stace, it's going to be okay."

"If you say so." The guard informed them that their visit was over. Derrick thought that it couldn't have been fifteen minutes that fast. Stacey told him to call her later on, and she left.

☐

Detective Howard informed Jenkins that Tee had several arrest, dating back to when he was a juvenile. A lot of his charges involved violence. His last known address was listed as 7525 E.75th Street. Also, prints from the car came back belonging to him.

"CIU faxed a picture of him along with all the information that they had pertaining to him."

"Looks like, he's been in trouble since he was a tyke." Jenkins said.

"Yeah it seems that way, so what are we going to do next?"

"Let's go and check this address and see what we can find out." They jumped in their unmarked car, and headed to an address that was located in Garden Valley.

Tee was still holed up in Kayla's apartment. He had been doing nothing but smoking weed and fucking her every chance that he got. He had been sending her out on errands, with the money that he got from the bank robbery.

Kayla was tired of him just laying up in her house. She couldn't stand to look him in the face, because every time he talked or smiled there was a big ass hole where his teeth used to be. Tee's cousin Tiffany had warned him that the police were looking for him. She didn't tell him that she was the one that gave them his name. Tee wanted to continue to lay low, but Kayla was ready for him to leave.

"So have you decided what you are going to do?"

"What you're in a rush for me to leave?"

"Well, you said you only needed a couple of days, and it's going on four days now."

"I been spending all my money on you, what you want some more?"

"That ain't it Tee, I don't want to get caught up in no bullshit. Now I done gave you a couple of days, it's time for you to move on."

"Bitches ain't shit. When a nigga on top y'all be on our dicks, but when we are down y'all don't want no parts of us."

"First I ain't no bitch, second all we been doing is fucking, so I don't owe you nothing."

"You right, I'll get up out of your spot tonight." He started thinking of other places that he may be able to stay.

28

Spaz, Crazy and T-Smooth were shook up after what happened to D-Nut. They were so nervous, that they didn't even strip Fred's car. Instead they drove it to an abandoned lot and burned it up. D-Nut's little sister kept coming around asking where he was at. They played dumb with her, as well as with the other set members. They knew that he was dead but didn't want to be linked to what happened to him.

D-Nut's mother filed a missing persons report. Three days later a detective showed up at her door.

"Mrs. Ervin, my name is Detective Martin and I have been assigned to investigate the missing person's report you filed concerning Darnell Ervin. That is your son, right?"

"Yes it is."

"May I come in?"

"Yes, come in." Mrs. Ervin had been dreading this day ever since her son had started hanging in the streets.

"Mrs. Ervin by any chance do you know if your son was involved in some type of gang?"

"Well he has a group of friends that he hangs with, but I wouldn't call them a gang."

"I have a picture that I would like to show you. It could be painful, so would you please take a seat?" She sat down and he gave her the picture. She took one look, dropped the picture to the floor and fell over screaming.

"They killed my baby! Oh, Lord he's dead." Detective Martin rushed over to console her.

"Is there anybody that you could call to be with you at this time?"

"My daughter will be home from school soon," she said in between sobs.

"You are going to have to go down to the city morgue to give a positive identification of the body. Also I need to ask you a few questions, okay?"

"Could you give me a minute to get myself together?" she asked as she got up to go into the bathroom to clean herself up. Once she got herself together as best she could, she went back out into the living room.

"Mrs. Ervin do you know any reason why your son would be down in the Garden Valley housing projects?"

"No I do not, is that where he was killed at?"

"That is where his body was found. Now I'm going to need you to give me the names and the whereabouts of the guys that he frequently hung with. They may be able to shed some light on what happened to him."

"I'm not familiar with any of the boy's names, but my daughter can help you out once she comes home."

"That would be fine. I can talk to her and drive you down town to ID his body." They sat and waited for her daughter to return from school. Mrs. Ervin offered him something to drink. He accepted water. Tanishia came into the house and instantly knew that something was wrong. She saw a man sitting on the couch in a too tight suit, and her mother sitting in the chair with her face stained with tears and her make up smeared.

She ran over to her mother, "What's wrong, ma?"

"It's Darnell, they killed my baby!" she said and started crying all over again. Tanishia and her brother were close. She was worried about him when she hadn't seen him in a couple of days. That's why she kept going up to where he hung out asking his friends if they had seen him. They told her no, but she felt like they were lying.

"Nishia we have to go down to the morgue to identify the body, and this man would like to ask you some questions."

"Tanishia my name is Detective Martin and I would like to ask you a few questions that may help us to determine what happened to your brother, can you help me?"

"I will try."

"That's good enough. Now do you know the names of the people that your brother hung around with?"

"I know them by their gang names."

"What gang are they in?"

"They're Bloods."

"And what are their names?"

"Crazy, T-Smooth and Spaz."

"And do you know where any of them stay at?"

"No, but I know where they hang out at."

"Would you look through some pictures for us, to see if you might be able to identify them for us?"

"Yes, I can do that."

"Okay are you ready to go?" he asked Mrs. Ervin.

"Yes." She said weakly.

Detective Martin took them to the morgue to identify the body. After that he took them to the station and a detective from the gang division brought over a photo book that contained pictures of all active Blood members that were on file. He had Tanishia look through the book. She came across a photo of a guy she knew as Crazy, and said that her brother hung out with him daily. Below the picture, was the name Carlton Baines. The gang detective identified him as a member of the MOB set of Bloods out of East Cleveland. Martin felt his adrenaline pumping. He knew he was close to solving the case. The only problem was Detective Jenkins was the lead investigator. He had to get approval from him on every move that he made, that frustrated him. He got an address on Baines and went to drop off Mrs. Ervin and her daughter.

☐

Sean called Linda, "I told you that I was going to call you."

"Yes you did, so what's up? Is you coming to get me?"

"Yeah, I'm going to swoop down there about eight o'clock, give me your address."

"Am I staying out over night?" she asked.

"That all depends on you."

"Okay I will be ready." they said their goodbyes and hung up. Then Linda called man. "Are you ready?"

"What's the deal?"

"He is coming to pick me up at eight, from my house."

"We will be there."

"Don't forget you owe me, too."

"Don't worry I got you, see you later." He hung up from her and called Jerrel.

"Rel get Tez and Ray Ray and get over here quick, we got that nigga."

An hour later Man and his cousins were sitting in a car parked down the street from Linda's house. They each had a weapon and a mask. It was decided that Tez and Man would take care of Sean.

At 8:20 Sean pulled up in Linda's driveway, and called her on the phone letting her know that he was outside. When they saw him pull up Man and Tez got out of the car, and crept on the side of the house. After a few minutes she came out. As she approached his car two figures crept from the side of the house. As soon as Linda opened his car door the interior light came on and Tez and Man started shooting. Sean never had a chance. He was shot in the face and chest numerous times. Linda turned and started running back towards her house when the shooting started. She made it to the top of the steps before she was thrown to the ground from a slug hitting her in the back. One of the masked men ran up on the porch and shot her in the head at point blank range. The two of them took off running back to the car, where the other two men were waiting.

"Damn Tez, you ain't have to shoot the bitch!" Man said to him.

"No witnesses no case. That bitch crossed that nigga, so who's to say that she wouldn't have crossed you. Ain't no loose ends, so we are good. We won't speak on this shit ever again." Once they got back to Man's house, Tez, Jerrel and Ray Ray went their separate ways.

29

Back in Miami, Spank and Tink were sitting in Spank's room smoking a blunt when Tink asked, "So have you talked to Allen?"

"No, but he should of met up with Sean and got the last of the dope."

"What about Sean? How has he been holding up?"

"He's cool, he been laying low at his girl's house. He said that he hadn't heard his name being linked to any shooting, so he's good."

"What about the Valley?"

"I heard that homicide still been down there sweating niggas."

"Tink, look man I ain't trying to think about what's going on in Cleveland right now. I got a date with the girl of my dreams, and I'm trying to have fun in the sun."

"Alright, me and Coco are about to go down to the hotel's pool. I will get up with you."

Spank got dressed and left to pick up Cherry. She shared a little condo with one of her girlfriends in downtown Miami. Cherry met Spank down in the parking garage.

"So what's on the agenda for today?"

"Well, first we are going sightseeing." she told him. She had him punch the destination into the GPS and he started driving. They ended up out in Seminole County, which had a beautiful view of the countryside. It had beautiful trees and green pastures. They parked the car got out and walked. Cherry told him that she comes out there to enjoy the peace and quiet. There was no sign of city life for miles around.

"Yeah it is peaceful out here." Spank agreed.

Cherry grabbed his hand and they continued to walk. "So where are you from?" she asked.

"I'm from Cleveland, Ohio."

"A mid westerner, huh?"

"Yeah, but we don't wear cowboy boots or ride horses."

"So what are you seeking from me, knowing that we are from two different places?"

"Honestly, I'm just looking to have a good time. Maybe have some new experiences that leave me with some good memories."

"Well, at least you're honest, I have to watch you."

"Why is that?"

"I could see myself falling for you. I feel comfortable and safe with you."

"I'm glad to hear that. Who knows what the future may hold. Let's just see where it takes us" he said to her as he leaned in and kissed her. Her lips were soft and juicy, and she closed her eyes and enjoyed the moment. When she felt his hand on her ass, she broke off the kiss.

"You move fast don't you?"

"It's hard to control myself with someone like you."

"Well, it's time for us to move on." The next destination that she had him punch into the GPS led them to Ester's, which was an upscale restaurant. They had a few drinks, and then she asked, "What is your real name? I don't like calling you Spank."

"It's Shamar."

"That's a nice name. That's who I would like to get to know."

"There is no difference, I stay one hundred."

"And what does that mean?"

"It means that I keep it real, I don't change."

"So are you a thug through and through?"

"What gives you the impression that I'm a thug?"

"Your whole demeanor, the way that you carry yourself. How can you show love and give it, if you're always hard?"

"I guess there's a time and place for everything."

"I know that you see me as a stripper, but I do have goals and aspirations. I do want to have a career one day. Do you have any goals?"

"Why are you getting so deep on me?"

"I'm just trying to get to know you. Is something wrong with that?"

"Not at all, let's see I would like to own my own business one day, and I would like to settle down and have kids."

"That's interesting, because you don't seem like the type."

"You have a lot to learn about me then."

"It's too much to learn in so little time."

"We got to make every minute count. Stay with me tonight, and we can keep learning about one another."

"I told you that I would have to watch you, you are very slick."

"I'm not slick, I'm just me. You are a beautiful lady, and if I never see you again, I want to experience something with you that will stay with me forever."

"And if I do stay with you, what will you be expecting?"

"Nothing that you aren't willing to do."

"Can you take me home so that I can pick up few things?"

"I will take you to buy the things that you need."

"Okay I'm with you for the night."

They left and road out to the mall, where he let her get a few toiletries and an outfit for the next day. Once they got back to the hotel he ordered Champagne from room service. They then decided to get into the hot tub. Spank felt like he was a God, and couldn't wait for the real games to begin.

☐

Back in Cleveland Sean and Linda's murder was broadcasted on the local news. Silvia seen it and called Allen and told him to turn on the news. Allen missed the first broadcast, but caught the second one. He couldn't believe it, he had just talked to Sean. He wondered if it was another robbery or retaliation for what had happened up in Morris Black. He knew that he had to get in touch with Spank, to let him know what happened. He called Spank three times and his phone kept going to voice mail. So he tried Tink's phone and he answered, "What's up?"

"Tink this Allen look, Sean got murked, it's all on the news."

"What! I thought he was laying low?"

"He was, but somebody got him. He was at Coco's friend Linda's house, they got her too. I tried calling Spank but his phone kept going to voice mail. I figured that I had to let you niggas know what happened."

"Look I'm about to go and holla at Spank. See what else you can find out and get back with us."

"Okay I'll do that." Tink hung up the phone and had a terrible look on his face. Coco noticed his mood and asked. "Baby what's wrong?"

"Baby I'm sorry to tell you this, but Linda got killed."

"You're lying!" she said as she started to get choked up.

"It's true baby, they killed Sean too."

"What were they doing together?"

"I don't know, Allen just called and told me that. He is about to try and find out more details and call me back. I got to call Spank right quick. He went and knocked on the door, and didn't get an answer. He tried the doorknob, the door was locked. He started banging on the door and calling Spank's name. Finally, he opened the door wrapped in only a towel. He was mad as hell, having been interrupted while he was ball deep in Cherry. He frowned at Tink, "What's up?"

"I just got a call from Allen telling me that Sean got smoked."

"Get the fuck out of here, he had the re-up money. They didn't rob him for it did they?"

Tink just shook his head. Here it was, he was telling him that Sean got killed, and all he wanted to know was did they get the money.

"Don't know, he just told me that he was at Coco's friend Linda's house and that they killed her too."

"Fuck, that shit don't sound right. There has to be more to it."

"Allen suppose to try and find out more details and get back with us. So what do you want to do, stay out here or catch a flight back?"

"Let's wait to hear back from Allen, before we make that decision."

"Okay then." Tink replied and then he walked back into his room. Coco was curled up on the bed crying. She and Linda had their little dispute, but that still was her girl. Tink laid on the bed next to her, and wrapped his arms around her. Coco sat up and turned to Tink, "I think it is time, for you to get out of the dope game. You have money saved up, invest it, or start a business. It's starting to get really dangerous."

"I understand that, but I can't just up and stop like that."

"Why can't you?"

"Because it's not that simple. Give me some time and we will figure it out, okay?"

"I'm going back, I want to attend her funeral."

"Let's just wait to hear back from Allen. Depending on what he says, I might be going back with you. So let's get a good night sleep and see what happens tomorrow. They curled up, and Coco fell asleep in his arms.

After hearing the news, Spank went and got right back in the bed with Cherry. He wasn't about to let anything come between experiencing everything that he could sexually with her. Her body was so beautiful, her pussy hair was the same texture as the hair that flowed from her head. He sucked every part of her body including her toes and asshole. Cherry thought damn he's a freak. They didn't stop sexing until four in the morning. They were so worn out, that they fell asleep nude without any covers on them.

30

The attorney that Derrick's parents hired for him went to visit him. His name was Mark Freidman. Attorneys received special visits with their clients. Derrick and his lawyer were placed in an interview room so that they could have their privacy. Derrick was brought into the room. Mark Freidman rose up out of his chair.

"How are you Derrick? My name is Mark Freidman, and I have been hired by your parents, to represent you." They shook hands and took a seat. Freidman opened his briefcase and removed a writing tablet and an ink pen.

"Well I went over the court documents, and I see that they have you charged with complicity to aggravated robbery and murder. Your father informed me that you wish to have your bond reduced. I'm going to tell you right now, that it's going to be very hard to do. I need you to give me the details of what happened."

Derrick told the attorney what happened, and to the attorney it seemed that either Derrick was the most naive person that he had ever met or that he was lying. The only thing that Derrick truly had going for him, was that he never entered the bank, nor was he the getaway driver. If he was part of the robbery, he would have done more than just sat in the passenger seat of the car. He was hired to represent Derrick, and he was going to do that to the fullest. He was going to point those facts out in his motion for a bond reduction.

He told Derrick that he would talk to the detectives on the case, file a motion for a bond reduction and get back with him in a couple of days. Freidman left and went back to his office. He went through the arrest report and saw that a detective Jenkins from homicide made the arrest, so he picked up the phone to call him.

Jenkins advised Mark Friedman that they had identified the shooter, and that he felt that if his client was so innocent, he wouldn't have refused to cooperate. Freidman told him that he would be seeking a bond reduction, since Derrick had no prior record and his family was willing to put up their house. Jenkins let it be known that he had nothing to do with that. It was between Freidman, the prosecutor and the judge.

A couple days later Freidman went back to visit Derrick.

"Well, Derrick I have good news and I have bad news. The bad news is that the judge denied the motion for the bond reduction. The good news is that they have identified the shooter. So, there is no need for you to keep withholding that information."

"If they know who he is then he will clear my name."

"That may be true, but it looks as if you're going to have to sit in here until that happens."

"If that's what it takes, then that's it."

"I'm going to draw up another motion to reduce your bond and see what happens."

"Yeah you do that." Derrick got up, and was escorted back to his pod. He thought that it would only be a matter of time, before they got Tee. He felt in his heart that Tee was going to clear him.

☐

Detective Martin went out to the address that Crazy resided at. He parked and conducted surveillance on the house. Around one o'clock a black male fitting Crazy's description exited the house. He got in a car and drove off with Martin following him. He drove three blocks then pulled to the curb in front of a corner store. Martin watched as the male exited the car and approached two other males. He gave them embraces and they started to chat. Martin pulled out his camera, and unbeknownst to them started snapping pictures. He was going to take the pictures to Tanishia to see if she could put names to the faces. Once he was finished he headed to the station.

The captain had called another emergency meeting. When Martin got to the station, Jenkins and Howard were also there standing outside of the conference room. The captain opened the door and told them to step in. They were surprised to see that the Mayor and a city councilman were present. The Captain told them to have a seat, then he began.

"Gentlemen we need to use swift measures in dealing with the violence that is plaguing our city. Last night two more people were shot and killed. A man and a woman. That's five dead bodies in three days, with no answers or arrest, Jenkins what is the problem?"

"Captain we are under staffed. There is only myself, Howard and Martin working these cases. The three of us have made progress in solving two of the cases, but we are going to need more manpower."

Howard jumped in, "Captain we have a positive identification on the suspect from the First Merit bank shooting, and it's only a matter of time before he is arrested, also Martin has been able to identify the man that was found dead down in Garden Valley. He also has tracked down some of his known associates. So you see we are making progress, we just need more manpower."

The Mayor asked the captain if he could say a few words, and was told to go right ahead.

"Gentlemen on behalf of the city I would like to thank you for the hard work that you have been putting in. I know that it is a tedious job. The captain is going to provide you with the manpower that is needed to solve these cases. Now if conventional tactics don't work, you're going to have to shake this city up. By that I mean pick up and harass every known criminal in this city until you get answers and make a point, am I understood?" They shook their heads in agreement.

"Martin," Captain says, "I'm going to assign another detective to work with you, and you will take over as lead detective on the Garden Valley case. Jenkins and Howard you two keep working on the First Merit bank and Morris Black cases. I'm going to assign Detectives Cooper and Watson to the case involving the man and woman that were killed last night."

"So is everything clear?"

"Yes sir."

"Everybody is dismissed, and gentlemen, no more excuses."

Howard asked Jenkins what the next move would be. The key bank case is already in the bag, so let's shoot up to Saint Luke's and see what we can learn about the Morris Black case." Martin met up with his new partner, whose name was Sanchez. The first thing they did was to visit Tanisha Ervin. She identified the other individuals in the pictures as Spaz and T-Smooth. Next they went back down to the gang unit and went through the picture book. They found what they were looking for, both of them were in the book. T-Smooth was listed as Terrance Howard and Spaz was listed as Michael Thompson.

They ran their names along with Crazy's and found out that their M/O was car theft and carjacking.

"Maybe it was a carjacking gone bad." Sanchez said.

"Call auto theft and see if they have any reports of any carjacking within the last week, especially in the Garden Valley area." Martin told him. Sanchez called down to auto theft, and fifteen minutes later he got off the phone and said, "I think we got something."

"What did you come up with?"

"There was a carjacking reported on the same day of the shooting. A Fred Sanders was interviewed at Saint Luke's hospital by Jenkins, after he had been shot in the hand and leg."

"You think he could be our perp?"

"It's possible, if not he may have some information that may lead us in the right direction."

"Was there an address listed in the report?"

"Yes, there is an address and a phone number listed."

"Well, let's go and check on this Fred Sanders." said Martin.

They went to the address and talked to Fred's mother, who informed them that Fred no longer lived there. Martin left his card advising her to call him. As soon as they left Fred's mother called his new cell phone and when he answered she said, "Boy I don't know what you have done, but some detectives came here looking for you. They were asking about your car."

"They probably found it, that's all."

"They left a number with me, and told me to have you call them."

"Give me the number." he got the number then hung up.

Fred called the number that his mother gave him. When someone answered the phone he read the name off of the card," I'm trying to reach detective Martin. He was placed on hold while his call was being transferred.

"This is Detective Martin speaking."

"This is Fred Sanders. You left your number with my mother for me to call you."

"Yes, can you come down to the station? I would like to ask you a few questions about the carjacking."

"I have to wait for my girl to get off of work to give me a ride."

"And what time will that be?'

"She gets off at four."

"Will six be okay then?"

"Yeah, that will be fine."

"See you at six Mr. Sanders. Fred hung up and started to wonder what they wanted to talk to him about. When Shannon got home, he had her take him down there. Inside the police station, he informed the desk clerk that he was there to see Detective Martin and was told to take the elevator to the fourth floor and make a right. He did as he was told, and was shocked to see that the sign above the door said Homicide Division. He went through the door and told the person at the desk there that he was there to see Detective Martin. A few minutes later, a tall white man came and led Fred into one of the interview rooms. Waiting inside was a Spanish looking man, who introduced himself as detective Sanchez. Martin told him to have a seat. Fred sat down and the interview began, with Martin asking questions.

"Mr. Sanders on June 10th you reported that you had been shot and carjacked, is that right?"

"Yes it is."

"Were you the only one shot?"

"As far as I know, yeah."

"Could you explain to us what happened?"

"I pulled up to a red light, and was hit from behind by another car. When I got out to check the damage, I noticed that there were two people in the other car. The driver got out approached me, told me he had insurance, and that he was going back to his car to get the paperwork. I went back to my car to get a pen, and while I was looking in my glove compartment another person sneaked up on me with a gun. He told me that it was a carjacking. I went for his gun and he shot me in the hand. I took off running, at which time he shot me in the leg."

"And what did you do after that?"

"I ran until I seen some people sitting on their porch, and I asked them to help me. They took me into their house and called an ambulance."

"Do you remember the people's name and address?"

"The old lady's name is Mrs. Pearl and her address is 7426 E.75th."

Martin and Sanchez exchanged glances. They knew that if his alibi was good that he couldn't be their perp. Martin asked if he could show him a few pictures, and he said yes. They showed him four pictures, and he identified Crazy as the driver of the car that hit him and D-Nut as the one that shot and carjacked him. Fred asked them, "Have y'all found my car yet?"

"No we haven't located it yet, but do you remember what time it was that the incident took place?"

"It happened about four o'clock."

Martin ended the interview, telling Fred that they would contact him if they needed any more information. After Fred left, Martin said to Sanchez, "The victim was killed around 6:45PM."

"That gave them enough time to stash his car, and go back to find another victim."

"Only their next victim wasn't so naïve." said Martin.

"Well we definitely know that Carlton Baines was with him that day."

"I say we pick them all up, put them against each other, and see if one will break. We can at least hold Baines on the carjacking charge."

Martin told Sanchez, "I'm going to try to get an arrest warrant for Baines on suspicion of carjacking. I want you to contact the East Cleveland PD. See if they have come across the vehicle."

"That's a good idea." said Sanchez as he reached for the phone.

31

Jenkins and Howard went up to Saint Luke's hospital. First they went to visit Rick. They asked him what happened. "We got robbed, a guy pulled up in a car approached us pretending that he was looking for someone, and then he pulled out a gun and robbed us."

Jenkins asked, "Did you resist when he tried to rob the two of you?"

"No, we emptied out our pockets."

"Then why do you think he shot you?"

"I don't know."

"Well, was he by himself?"

"There was a girl sitting in his car."

"Can you describe the person that shot you?"

"He was short, dark skinned and kind of chubby."

"And what type of car was he driving?"

"I just know that it was a black car."

"Okay Mr. Harris, if we have any more questions we'll contact you."

They went out into the hallway, and Howard asked, "Do you think that he is telling the truth?"

"I doubt it, it just doesn't sound right." Howard said.

"There was a girl that was shot, and admitted on the same day as him."

"Do you know her name?"

"Yes, her name is Nena Miles and she is in room 314 on the third floor."

"Well let's make our way down there."

Rick did not cooperate with them, because he knew that if the truth came out he would end up getting charged. He also wanted to let the streets deal with Sean. It was his actions that led to his present condition but he still blamed Sean.

Jenkins and Howard entered Nena's room. She looked up, and wondered what they wanted. "Ms. Miles my name is Detective Jenkins and this is Detective Howard. We are investigating your shooting. Could you please tell us what happened?"

"I guess I got hit by a stray bullet."

"Why do you think it was a stray bullet?"

"Because I did not see anybody, I was at the bus stop and heard gunshots. I got hit and woke up in here."

"Were you by yourself at the bus stop?"

"Yeah, I was waiting to catch the bus to a friend's house.

"And what bus stop were you at?"

"The one on 93rd and Hough."

"One last question, you weren't by chance up in Morris Black housing projects at any time on that day were you?"

"No, I was not. I don't know anybody up there."

"Okay thank you for your time Ms. Miles. If you can think of anything else that may be helpful, please contact us at this number." Jenkins told her and handed her a card. They left, and on the way to the car Jenkins said, "I don't believe her story either. They are both withholding something."

"Without any proof, what can we do?"

"Let's go back and talk to the vic's mother. Maybe she can shed some new light on what happened." They got in the car and headed for Tone's Mother's house. The East Cleveland PD advised Sanchez that a car matching the description he gave, was found burned in an abandoned lot. He told him that most of the inside was burned, but the outside was still intact. He told Sanchez what impound lot the car was in. Sanchez went to the pound and dusted the car for prints, and wrote down the VIN number. He ran a check, and the car came back registered to Fred Sanders. Several prints came back off of the car, with one set belonging to Carlton Baines. Sanchez said to his self, "Bingo!"

Martin secured an arrest warrant for Crazy, and assembled a team to implement it. They were going after Crazy, T-Smooth and Spaz. They selected a staging point, and then Martin and Howard went and conducted surveillance at the same store where the pictures were taken. They did not have to wait long, within twenty minutes Crazy pulled up with Spaz and T-Smooth in the car with him. Martin radioed for the team to move in.

The police came swarming from different directions. T-Smooth, who was in the front passenger seat seen them coming and jumped out of the car. He took off running, with two officers fast on his heels. He knew the neighborhood like the back of his hand, all he needed was a little space to lose them. His Tech 9 was hanging off of his shoulder under his jacket. He grabbed it with his right hand and started shooting behind him, the officers dove to the ground. T-Smooth then cut through a backyard and began jumping fences. By the time the police had surrounded the area he was long gone.

Spaz and Crazy were taken down to the station, and put in two different rooms. Martin decided that they would work on Spaz first. They entered the interrogation room, and Martin spoke, "So Mr. Thompson are you going to let Mr. Baines put the murder charge on you?"

"What are you talking about?"

"Well your friend Baines implicated you in the death of your friend Darnel Ervin."

"What! You're lying."

"He said you and Ervin were involved in a carjacking that went bad, down in Garden Valley. Now whether you know it or not when more than one person engages in criminal activity which leads to one of their deaths, the other party becomes responsible for their death. They usually are charged with voluntary manslaughter, which carries ten to twenty five years. So I want you to think very carefully before you start lying." Spaz didn't believe that Crazy tried to pin what happened to D-Nut on him. There was no way that he could do it without implicating his self. Spaz decided that they were running game, and he wasn't about to be tricked.

"I don't know what y'all are talking about, and I would like to call my attorney."

"You want to play hardball Mr. Thompson? We won't give you any breaks later."

"Like I said I would like to call my lawyer. I have nothing else to say to y'all."

They left out of the room. Martin said, "On to the next one." They then entered the room that held Crazy and the same game began.

Jenkins spoke "Mr. Baines, I guess the code of silence with gang bangers don't exist anymore."

"What the hell are you talking about?"

"Well your friend next door gave you up so easily, that's hard to believe that you actually considered him your friend." Crazy started getting nervous.

"What did he tell y'all?"

"That you are responsible for your friend Darnell Ervin's murder."

"I ain't killed nobody!"

"That may be true to a certain extent, but you participated in a carjacking that left one man with two gunshot wounds and another that left your friend dead. So before you say anything let me give you all the evidence that is stacked against you. Number one the guy that you two carjacked for the Cutlass has positively identified you. Two the car that y'all burned up, only burned on the inside. Your prints were lifted from the outside door handle, and three your friend next door said that you were there when Ervin got killed."

"I ain't going down like that. Did he tell y'all that he was there too?"

"Slow down Mr. Baines, here is the deal we want the guy that killed your friend. You help us get him and we will help you."

"He was in a black BMW 745."

"Start from the top and tell us what happened." Crazy told them how they had been laying on the car, when the commotion started at the basketball court. He continued to say a guy quickly jumped in the BMW that is when they followed him, and bumped his car when he stopped at the light. He told them that the guy must of knew that something was up because he jumped out of his car, with a gun in his hand and started shooting. He even told them that T-smooth started shooting the Tech through the windshield so that they could get away. He shot the BMW up when they were pulling off. He described the guy as a tall dark skinned dude that had on basketball shorts.

Crazy asked, "What are y'all charging me with?"

"As of now you are being charged with complicity to carjacking and assault. We have to talk to the DA to see what we can work out for you. Give us a couple of days. We may also need you to look at some pictures for us, to help us identify the person that you are talking about."

They left out of the room, and Sanchez said "Your good man, how did you know that he would break?"

"The odds, it's the odds that one out of two always turn." They went back in the room that held Spaz, and Jenkins said, "You will be transferred to County jail, and you can call your attorney when you get there. Tell him that you are being charged with attempted aggravated robbery and voluntary manslaughter. The first time I was bluffing, but your partner is not as strong as you. We know the whole story, so sit in the County and understand how it feels to stand strong for someone that betrays you."

They left and Jenkins told Sanchez, "We got to go back to Garden Valley. We have to find out who drives that BMW. Crazy and Spaz were both cuffed and put in a van to be transferred to the county. They both cursed each other, calling each other a snitch. Spaz vowed to kill Crazy if he ever get close enough to him.

☐

Jenkins did not do any better with Tone's mother. She said that she did not know anything, and was waiting on them to provide her with answers. The other detectives that were assigned to Sean and Linda's case were unsuccessful as well. They couldn't find one witness.

32

Allen put his ear to the street, but couldn't find out anything about what happened to Sean and Linda. The police did not even have any suspects. He called Spank to give him the update. Spank told him that they would be back in Cleveland the next day, and to pick them up from the airport.

Sean had enough of their money to buy ten keys, and Spank wanted the money or the keys. He told Tink to book their flight, and he called Cherry. He told her that he needed to see her, but she told him that she had to work. He decided that he would go up to her job. He went to the strip club and got the same seat that he had the first night when he first met Cherry. It did not take long for Cherry to appear.

"Do you want a dance?" she asked.

"How about we go into the VIP section, for a little more privacy?"

"It cost a hundred dollars to enter."

"Money is no object when it comes to spending time with you."

"This way then," she said as she grabbed his hand and led the way.

They went into the VIP section, and entered a private room that had a couch and a cocktail table. Spank sat down and she knelt before him. He told her, "Baby girl something important has come up back home and I have to fly back tomorrow."

"So I guess this will be my last time seeing you?"

"I doubt it, as soon as I straighten things out I plan on coming back. Until then we can stay in touch."

"I guess we can do that."

"Don't be sad baby girl, let's just make every moment count." he said to her as he stood up and dropped his pants. Cherry took him into her mouth. The feeling felt so good, that he was ready to ask her to come back to Cleveland with him. He wanted to be up in her, so he pulled out of her mouth, stood up and bent her over the couch. He slid her thong to the side and entered her. First, he slow stroked her, just enjoying the feeling. While he was fucking her he started thinking about all of the problems that he had been having. Trying to let out his frustration, he started pounding her as if there was no tomorrow. He busted off in her raw, then fixed his clothes. He told her that he would call her when he touched down in Cleveland.

Cherry thought that it was just another dream being sold. She got herself together and went back to work.

☐

Spank and Tink touched back down in Cleveland at Hopkins International Airport. Allen was there to pick them up. Spank started right in.

"What's the word? Have you heard anything yet?"

"Spank, the streets ain't talking. Don't nobody know nothing."

"That's bullshit! That nigga had two hundred and fifty thousand dollars of mine and I want it."

"Well I don't think he had it on him when he got murked, because they ain't mention anything about it on the news."

"Then it can't be but at one of two places, either his mother's house or his girl's house."

Coco and Tink were tripping, they couldn't believe that Spank was more concerned about the money, than the death of his friend. Coco felt that he did not care about Tink either, and wished that he would break away from him.

Tink told Allen to drop him off at Coco's house. Spank said, "We can drop her off, but we got business to tend to." Coco couldn't hold her tongue any longer.

"Spank you are so selfish."

"Self-preservation baby girl."

"You are going to grow old by yourself, watch!"

"Tink, check your girl, my nigga."

"Chill baby, I'll be back as soon as we find out what's going on." Tink said.

"You are going to end up dead or in jail fucking with that nigga. He don't care about you."

"Since you talking all that shit, why ain't you tell him how I seen him blowing your back out, and you ain't say shit?" Spank broke in.

"Fuck is you talking about?" asked Tink.

The night that I went to the club, when I came back I came to your room to holla at you. When I opened the door you was hitting her from the back with your eyes closed, but she looked me dead in the eyes and didn't say shit, I just closed the door."

"He's a damn liar!" Coco said.

"Listen fuck all the bullshit. It's too much going on right now. We are about to drop you off and I will see you later." Tink told Coco.

Tink turned to Spank, "You my dawg, but don't ever try to plant no seeds in my head about my bitch. She has been down with me way before me and you met. She was down with me when I ain't had shit. So man to man don't play me like that no more Spank." Spank knew how Tink felt about Coco, and knew that he was serious, so he just let it go.

"My bad homie, can we just focus on the task at hand?"

"And what is that supposed to be?"

"Finding out what happened to Sean and that money." Tink knew that Spank's only real concern was about that money.

Spank told Allen to drive them out to his house. He had a hideout spot out in Euclid. They went out there so that he could put his plans in effect.

He said, "Look we got to go up in Sean's mother's house and his girl's house. Allen do you remember where his girl stay at?"

"Yeah I think so."

"Why can't you wait until after the funeral?" asked Tink.

"Because I want that money before anybody else has a chance to get their hands on it."

The truth was Spank was nearly broke. He had less than twenty thousand dollars left to his name. He had been splurging heavily and without that money it was a wrap.

"So you just gonna run up in his mother's house?" asked Tink.

"We are going to go in there when she is not at home. If the safe is there, it's got to be in his room."

"So when are we supposed to do this?"

"Tomorrow, and if we don't find it at his mother's then we are going to shoot out to his girl's crib." They made plans on what time they were going to move the next day, and then Tink told Allen to take him to Coco's.

Tink trusted Coco, but he still couldn't get what Spank said out of his head. When he got to her house he confronted her, "You saw that nigga watching us fuck, and you ain't say shit?"

"When I looked up I just seen him closing the door. I didn't think it was a big deal, it was your ass that he could see not mine."

"You got jokes huh?"

"Tink are you going to let that nigga come between us. We been down with each other too long for this bullshit." Tink thought for a minute and realized that she was right. He had to get his mind right. He decided that when the shit was over that he was going to break away from Spank, and just be his own man.

□

The next day around ten o'clock Spank and Allen picked Tink up, and they headed to Sean's mother's house.

"Y'all ain't go believe this. That hoe Nanky that be with Spud tried to rob me." Allen said.

"Get the fuck out of here!" said Spank.

"I kid you not, I took that bitch to the hotel, fucked her and passed out. The bitch rolled my pockets and took my car keys. I caught the bitch in my trunk."

"What did you do to her?" asked Spank.

"I left that bitch unconscious in that hotel room."

"That's my dawg." Spank told him and gave him dap.

"We play bitches they don't play us." he said and looked at Tink with a smirk.

They pulled up to the house and Spank and Allen got out. Spank knew what room belonged to Sean. Allen took a crow bar out of his trunk and gave it to him to pry the window open. They climbed inside while Tink was the lookout. He refused to break into his dead friend's mother's house. They ransacked his room and found nothing. Spank decided that they should search the whole house. They were in the house over an hour and found nothing.

"It took y'all over an hour to search his room?" Tink said.

Spank just looked at him and told Allen to drive out to the girl's house. He wasn't going to give the girl as much respect as he did Sean's mother. Once they got to the girl's house, Spank threw Allen a ski mask and they got out of the car. They went up to the house and Spank knocked on the door, and some one answered, "Who is it?"

"Delivery," Spank said.

"Hold on a second." said the voice. Spank and Allen pulled their masks down over their faces, and when she opened the door they stormed into the house. Spank slapped her with the pistol, and then put her in a choke hold. He whispered in her ear, "I know that money is here. Now if you act dumb I'm going to kill you, but if you just give me the money we won't hurt you. Nod your head if you understand me." She nodded her head.

Spank continued, "Now I'm going to uncover your mouth and I want you to take me to the money okay?" She nodded her head again.

Spank took his hand off of her mouth, and she led them into the bedroom and showed them the safe that was stashed in the closet. Spank tied her up, then he and Allen struggled with the safe, carrying it out to the car. They put the safe in the trunk, and headed to Spank's house. Once there, they carried the safe into the basement. It was a heavy duty safe, and was not going to be easy to open. They were going to have to find an expert to get into it.

Spank felt relieved. He did not care that the safe was locked, all that mattered was that it was in his possession. He asked Allen, "How much dope do you got left?"

"I got a bird and a half left, the rest has been distributed. I think I got like forty grand also."

"So we are good until I can get this thing opened?"

"Yeah, we are good." Allen told him.

"Shoot me back down to the hood, Allen." Tink said

"What are you going to do?" Allen asked Spank.

"I'm going to chill out here. I got to see about getting this safe opened and getting my car fixed. I will call you, when I get through with everything, so that you can come and get me."

"Alright then, we are out." Allen and Tink headed down to Longwood.

33

Sean and Linda's funerals were a day apart. Outside of Linda's family, Coco and Tink were the only ones that attended her funeral. Sean's was a different story. He was well known and people came from all over Cleveland to attend his funeral. So many people attended that there wasn't enough seating. People had to stand along the walls. After his funeral Longwood had a cookout, and most of the people that knew Sean were in attendance.

Nena was out of the hospital, but she was on bed rest so she could not attend. She had gotten word of Sean's death and it had shaken her up pretty bad. In her heart she felt that it had to be retaliation for what had happened up in Morris Black. Sean did not have any enemies. She just couldn't understand why someone would want to hurt him, let alone kill him. At that point, she decided that she was done with the streets. She was going to go back to school and do something with her life.

Derrick's attorney went to see him again, with more bad news. Because the prosecutor told the judge that Derrick was refusing to cooperate, the judge refused to lower his bond. His decision to keep quiet put a strain on his and Stacey's relationship also. Whenever he called her or she came to visit him they argued.

She told him that one night she got off late after working overtime, that she thought she had seen Tee when she was getting off the bus. She tried to follow him, but lost him. She told Derrick that if she ever saw him again, that she was turning him in. Derrick told her to stay away from Tee. Derrick did not want to see any harm come her way. He had witnessed firsthand the violent side of Tee.

Derrick was touched to know that she cared about him. Derrick thought to himself when he got out he was going to marry her. He read the bible front to back. That helped him keep the faith and know that one day soon he would be released.

⬜

Martin and Sanchez made it hard for all the dope boys to make any money in the Valley. They cruised the blocks constantly, jumping out on them. They cornered a few and told them, "All we are trying to do is locate the driver of a black BMW. We do that and y'all can go back to your normal activities. We're homicide not vice." One guy yelled out of the crowd, "Go talk to Pam."

"And who is Pam?"

"The mother of the little girl that got shot at the courts." Sanchez and Martin walked back to their car.

"Do we have any information on the kid that was shot?" Sanchez asked.

"I think someone else interviewed the mother. We can pull up the report to get an address." They arrived at Pam's house and knocked on the door. Pam opened it and allowed them to come in. She really hated police, but she wanted justice for her baby. She was hoping that they were there to tell her that they had arrested the person that shot her daughter.

Martin began, "Ms. Sims we are investigating the shooting that happened at the courts, which led to your daughter being shot. Did you see who was shooting?"

"Shit, everybody was shooting. It sounded like a war out there, but to answer your question no I did not see who was shooting. I just took my baby up there to watch the game, and now she is wearing a shit bag."

"We understand your frustration. We are trying to get these guys off the streets. Would you happen to know the person that was driving a black BMW that day?" It was one of them Longwood fellas. I think the one that started the fight."

"And do you know his name?"

"I think it was Tank or Spank, something like that."

"Okay. Thank you for your time Ms. Sims, as soon as we catch who it was that shot your daughter we will notify you."

"Yeah, y'all do that," she let them out and closed the door. She had no faith in them and hoped that Dame and Disco would take care of who ever done that to her baby. Pam had no insurance so she was grateful that Dame was helping her with the things that Keisha needed.

Martin and Sanchez focused their attention on Longwood. They started riding through looking for a BMW. Sanchez said, "Baines told us that the BMW got shot up, so most likely it's being hidden or is in the shop getting repaired."

"Your right, we just need to get a tag on the person that owns it.

"Let's see if we can find something on a Tank or Spank from this area."

"We can check with the Gang Unit." said Sanchez.

"It won't be long before we have him." Martin said as he headed back towards the station.

☐

Spaz got in touch with T-Smooth and told him that Crazy had flipped. T-Smooth did not want to believe it.

"On everything blood, that nigga ratted on me. They ran game trying to put us against each other and he fell for it, and told them everything. It's going to come out in due time, you will see." Spaz told him.

"If it's true I'm going to handle that for you. I'm going to put the hood up on what's going down, too. Do you need anything?"

"No I'm good, I just wanted to put you up on what went down."

"Alright blood, if you hear more get at me." T-Smooth told him then hung up. He decided that he needed to blow Cleveland for a minute. He decided to shoot out to Lorain, Ohio where his cousins lived. It was a small quiet town, so if he stayed under the radar, he would be good. He packed some of his things then caught a cab down to the Greyhound Bus station.

☐

A week later, everything was back good for Spank. He had paid five grand to a guy from a security company to crack the safe. His car had been fixed and painted. To his surprise the safe was filled with dope. Sean had got a chance to re-up with the connect before he got murked. The safe had ten nicely stacked keys of cocaine in it.

Spank was ready to flood the city. He had the roof of his car open as he drove down to Longwood. He couldn't wait for the people to see that he was back, as if he truly ever went anywhere. He pulled up to Longwood's swimming pool, which was a popular hangout. All the fly honies would sit up at the benches, talk shit and drink. The dope boys would park their cars back to back, smoke and make deals. Spank got out of his car and all the fellas approached him, and gave him dap.

Detectives Martin and Sanchez were parked in the parking lot across the street from the pool. Martin had a camera equipped with a zoom lens. He snapped pictures for ten minutes, of the guys that were huddled around the BMW.

Spank stayed up at the pool for about a half an hour, and then said his goodbyes. He got in his car, drove around the block and pulled into a parking lot. He was going to pick up Tink. He got out of the car and walked up the walkway. When he was out of sight, Martin pulled up behind his car and wrote down the plate number. He then, pulled off using his best Sherlock Holmes's impersonation he said,

"Patience is a virtue, my dear Watson."

They went back to the station, where Martin had the film developed. While he was doing that Sanchez ran the plates off of the car. It came back registered to a Shamar James. Once the film was developed Martin told Sanchez, "Let's go, we are going over to the county." They went over to the county to visit Crazy. When he was brought in he was anxious to see what they had to say. He was hoping that they had good news for him.

"How are you doing Mr. Baines?" Martin asked.

"I would be a whole lot better, if y'all would let me out on bond."

"We are getting close to closing this case. You help us do that, and then we will help you. Now I would like to show you a few pictures and you tell me what you see."

He first was shown a picture of a group of men that were standing by a BMW. Crazy stared at the picture for a moment, and then pointed at a tall dark skinned person standing in the middle of the crowd.

"That's him right there, and that's the car minus the bullet holes." They showed him the picture of Spank by his self, "That's the same guy."

"Okay here is the deal. You're going to have to testify for us and we will push for the prosecutor to drop the charges against you down to attempted auto theft. You might get a year or two. That's the best we can do."

"What about my bond?"

"We will see that it is dropped to an amount that you can post."

"Okay then, deal." Crazy told him.

He just wanted to make bond, he had no intentions of sticking around. He was going down to Alabama with his son's mother.

The next day Martin drew up an arrest warrant for Spank's arrest. Crazy's charges were dropped down and his bond was lowered.

Crazy made bond, and on the way home stopped at the store where he hung out at. He bought a box of Black and Milds and a beer. T-Smooth had put the word out on the street that Crazy had snitched. One of the little homies seen Crazy enter and leave out of the store and called T-Smooth's cell phone.

"Hey Tee, that nigga Crazy is out."

"Are you sure lil homie?"

"I just watched the nigga go in and leave up out of the store, he just left the block."

"Good looking Blood and little homie keep this between us alright?"

"You know I got you big homey." T-Smooth hung up and asked his cousin could he borrow his car to make a run up to Cleveland right quick. He assured him that he wouldn't be gone no longer than a couple hours. His cousin told him to go ahead. T-Smooth stopped at a gas station and filled up then he jumped on the freeway. He couldn't let Crazy be a witness against Spaz and a potential witness against him. He made up his mind that Crazy had to take a permanent nap.

Martin and Sanchez got another team together and headed down to Longwood. They parked strategically throughout the projects, and waited for the signal. Around Five o'clock Spank pulled up in Coco's parking lot. Martin waited and a few minutes later Tink walked up and got in the car with him. Martin gave the signal. When Spank tried to pull out S.W.A.T. blocked him in. The car was surrounded before they even had a chance to think. They arrested Tink along with Spank. A search of the car revealed two keys of cocaine. If Spank had of spoken out on the spot about the dope, they would have let Tink go. They were taken to the station, where Spank was booked on suspicion of murder. They were just holding Tink under investigation hoping that they could find something on him. Martin and Sanchez tried to break him.

"Some friend you have, he wouldn't speak out for his own dope, that's why you're here. Now we don't want you, we want him. We believe that he was involved in a shooting that left a man dead. You help us with that and you can walk out of here."

"I don't know shit, I can't tell y'all nothing.'

"You know you can be charged with possessing that dope. Now are you going to stand up for a man that won't stand up for you?"

"I'm standing up for myself. I'm a man and intend to stay that way, now take me to my cell." Tink wasn't going out like no bitch. He knew he was good, but he was definitely going to deal with Spank's ass whenever they got out. Tink felt that Spank should have cut him loose on the spot. Their friendship was damaged forever.

34

T-Smooth pulled up in East Cleveland, and called Crazy's house from a pay phone.

"What's up blood?" T-Smooth said.

"Tee, what's up homie?"

"Shit, I heard that you was out, so I'm just checking up on you to see if you're alright."

"Tee, that nigga Spaz is foul. He ratted on me, blood."

"It's real my nigga, on the set."

"Look I'm going to come and swoop you. We are going to go to the Outback and have a good meal, and smoke some good shit."

"Alright, come on through."

"It's been hot since I shot at those cops. Meet me at the corner of your street. I'm in a black Camaro."

"Okay, what time?"

"I'll be there in twenty minutes."

"I'll be there!" Crazy said and hung up. He started packing his stuff because he planned to catch the Greyhound to Alabama the first thing in the morning. After he finished packing, he grabbed his coat and headed out the door. He walked up to the corner and waited about five minutes, before a black Iroc pulled to the curb in front of him. Crazy got in and T-Smooth passed him a blunt.

"Get your lungs right my nigga, I know your chest is empty."

"Thanks." Crazy said then took two long pulls off the blunt. His throat started to go numb.

"Is this bitch dipped?"

"You know it, I soaked that bitch." Crazy took two more pulls then passed it back to T-Smooth. He sat back in his seat as the effects of the wet began to hit him. T-Smooth smoked as he headed for the freeway. He turned to Crazy, "So what happened with you and Spaz?"

"He told on me plain and simple."

"What did he tell them?"

"That I was there when D-Nut jacked dude for the Cutlass, and that I was with D-Nut when he got killed." To make it sound good he said, "He told on you too. He told the people that you was shooting your Tech."

"The nigga told on me, too?"

"Hell yeah, he ain't right."

"So did he get out too?"

"T, he's probably in hiding somewhere."

They were riding down the highway when T-Smooth said, "I got to pull over and take a piss right quick." He pulled over on the side of the highway, where there was a deep embankment. He got out of the car and was pretending to take a leak. T-Smooth cocked his gun and got back in the car. He told Crazy to reach in the backseat and grab a bag for him off of the floor. Crazy turned around and grabbed the bag, when he turned back around in his seat, T-Smooth shot him in the head.

Crazy was slumped over in the front seat. T-Smooth got back out of the car and went around to the passenger's side. He opened the door and pulled Crazy out. He rolled him down the embankment, and for safe measures he went down there and shot him in the head again.

He wasn't going to tell anyone, not even Spaz. He would figure it out once he got released. T-Smooth got back in the car and headed back to Lorain.

☐

After Tee left Kayla's house, he roamed through the projects. He was staying with different friends. He would come out at night and rob the dope boys. They were hanging in groups late at night to protect each other. That didn't stop Tee, he would lay in the cut, watch and wait to catch them slipping. He did not care how many people were in a group. One night he was robbing a group of seven, when one of them went for a gun. Tee shot him in the jaw, and made a point, do not play with him. Everybody knew that he was on the run but, it was like he was a ghost. He only popped up at night, he was never seen in the daytime.

Late one night when he was casing the block he ran into Lucy. She used to be a dime back in the day. She got turned out on the water, and had been in a slow decline. She still looked pretty and had a body. She sparked Tee's interest and he approached her, "What are you doing out here this late by yourself?"

"I'm looking for a man."

"Well like Mystical said, the man is right here."

"Your funny, I like you."

"Well that makes two of us." he said and smiled.

"Do you get high?"

"Yeah on weed."

"You ain't never smoked no dip?"

"You talking about wet?"

"Yeah the wet, the skinny minny. That shit makes me freaky as hell."

"Well there is always a first time for everything, who got it?"

"You can get two sticks for thirty dollars from Jason."

"These niggas are kind of shook of me, I'm going to give you the money and you go get it."

"Give me the money," she said. He gave her the money, and she went and copped it. They walked together to her house. When they entered there were babies sleeping on the floor. There was a raggedy couch and a thirteen inch color TV sitting on a stand.

"Are those your kids?" he asked.

"One of them is, the other one is my nephew. My sister is asleep in the bedroom, so we got to be quiet. Let's go in my room."

They went in her room and she turned on a lamp. Her room was a mess and only had a mattress and box spring on the floor. Lucy kicked her shoes off, and grabbed a lighter off of her dresser. She fired up the dipped cigarette, and started smoking it. The smell made Tee want to throw up. He watched her smoke half of the cigarette, and thought damn she's greedy.

"Is you going to let me hit it?"

She handed it to him, and fired up the other one. She had a high tolerance, but Tee wasn't used to smoking wet. He started tripping, and told Lucy to take off her clothes. She slowly stripped off her clothes, and laid down on the bed. Tee stripped off his pants and boxer shorts, then climbed on the bed. He knelt in front of her and forced his dick in her mouth. Lucy was in a zone, and was stuck. Tee grabbed her head and pushed it up and down on his dick. He got tired of that so he spread her legs and started fucking her. She just laid there, it was like she wasn't even in the room. He fucked her hard but he still didn't get a response. The wet was kicking in, and he started hearing voices and hallucinating.

Tee called her the devil and said he knew that she was trying to kill him. He told her, "You can't feel it, huh? I got something for you!" he yelled as he rolled her onto her stomach. He sodomized her, yet she still did not respond. Tee got mad and started smacking her and yelling, "Bitch say something! Say something!" The yelling woke up her niece. She came out of her room and walked over to Lucy's room. Tee was in there throwing things and cursing, then he picked up his gun and started pistol whipping Lucy. Her niece ran over to the next door apartment, and started banging on the door. A lady opened the door, "What's wrong baby?"

"There is a man over there hurting my aunty!" she cried. The lady pulled her into the house, and called 911. It took over a half an hour for the police to show up. When they arrived, they had to kick in the bedroom door. Tee was passed out naked, clutching his gun, and Lucy was lying in a pool of blood on the bed. They couldn't tell if she was alive or dead, and quickly radioed for an ambulance.

Tee was cuffed and transported to Metro Hospital, and put on a psychiatric ward. The paramedics took Lucy to Charity Hospital. She had a concussion, a broken jaw and many lacerations, but she was okay. Tee stayed on the psychiatric ward for three days, and then he was transferred to the County jail. When his prints came back he was booked on numerous charges, including rape and murder. He still wasn't in his right state of mind. The water had taken him on a trip that he had yet to come back from.

35

Crazy's body was discovered, by work release inmates that were cleaning the side of the highway. It was two weeks before the body was found, and took another week for the body to be identified. Martin and Sanchez were notified, Martin knew that there was going to be hell. He turned to Sanchez and said, "There goes our case." He knew that more heat would be coming from the Mayor.

After seventy two hours they had to let Tink go, and now with Crazy dead Spank would walk on the murder charge, even though they still had him on the key of dope. Spaz would most likely walk too.

Sometimes Martin often wondered to himself was it even worth it. He thought he could make a change, when he first started his job. He came to the realization that there was never a real dent ever put in crime. As far as solving cases it was like the lottery, sometimes you win and sometimes you don't.

He caught flak from Captain Smith, for his handling of the case. He was given a chance to be a lead detective and he blew it, and it did not stop there.

Spank hired a high priced lawyer that got him off the drug charges on a technicality. Martin had obtained an arrest warrant, but he did not secure a search warrant. During the arrest the police were only allowed to conduct an incident to arrest search. Meaning that they were only allowed to search the area in which he had immediate access to. They weren't supposed to search the trunk without probable cause. Spank's lawyer filed a motion to suppress the evidence and the court ruled in his favor.

Spank walked out of the County jail a free man, and Martin felt deflated. Jenkins came out a little better. They got Tee and finally some leads in the double homicide case and the Morris Black case, thanks to an anonymous caller.

□

Man couldn't hold his tongue, he was up in the Black in a dice game, when he and a guy named June got in an argument. June felt that Man had fronted on him when Tone was alive, so he threw lugs at him.

"How are you making out, with your cousin gone?" He asked Man.

"What the fuck you mean by that?"

"Shit, you was like Superman when he was alive, all rah rah and shit."

"I stay the same, with someone or by myself."

"You sure ain't handled whoever it was that slumped your cousin. If somebody killed somebody in my family I would have been got at them."

"Why is you fucking with me fam? You got beef with me or something?"

"If I had beef with you, I would be at you. You need to have beef with that nigga that slumped your people."

"I been at him. Who you think slumped him and the bitch that was on the news?" Man said pulling his gun out. He started shooting at June, and he took off running. One of the bullets hit June in the ass. Everybody at the game was laughing when June started going in on Man, thinking it was funny. The mood changed when Man started busting his gun. They were quick to tell Man that it wasn't that serious. Some even tried telling him that he was wrong. Man wasn't trying to hear nothing. People thought he was sweet without Tone. He was going to show them he could stand on his own. "All y'all niggas drop down."

"You playing it like that man?" one of them asked.

"Yeah it's like that! Y'all are going to respect my gangsta, now empty them pockets." After that Man went on a one person robbing spree, but not being able to hold his water would prove to be a big mistake. June ended up making an anonymous call to the police telling them that Man was involved in the Morris Black killing and the double homicide involving the man and woman. He even told them that Man's real name was Marcus Mills.

Jenkins secured an arrest warrant, and they ran up in his aunt's house, but he wasn't there. His aunt called and told him that the police were looking for him, and he went into hiding. Man had to duck more than the police. Word got back to Jerrel and the rest of his cousins that he had ran his mouth. They weren't going to take a chance that he would hold up if he got knocked. They wanted him silenced. He quickly skipped town and went to Chicago and kept a low profile.

Jenkins refused to cut Derrick loose, even after they got Tee. Tee would not talk to the police, but he did write an affidavit for Derrick's attorney. The prosecutor was young and trying to make a name for his self. He told Derrick to either take a ten year plea or prepare for trial, and Derrick chose trial. His attorney asked him, "Derrick do you really want to chance going to trial, and having to trust that Tee would clear you?"

"It's a chance that I am going to have to take, because I ain't copping out."

The trial was set for two weeks later. Derrick had Stacey buy him a suit and some dress shoes to wear. Stacey did not trust all the praying that Derrick was doing would help clear him. She decided to take things into her own hands. She was almost three months pregnant, and if Derrick got sent away she was having an abortion. She decided to go and visit Tee, to make sure that he was going to do the right thing. She went down to the County, and he was brought out into the visiting room. He was surprised to see her. He sat down and picked up the receiver.

"What brings you down here Stacey?"

"Look Tee you're done, they got you. I am three months pregnant, I need my baby to have a father. Derrick did right by you and kept it real. Now I'm asking you to keep it gangsta and free him. He is going to trial, and putting his faith in you. For some reason he sees you as a true friend." She got choked up, started crying and said "Free him Tee."

He tapped on the glass and said, "I got you," then got up and walked away. Stacey did not even tell Derrick about what she did. She just prayed that Tee would keep it real.

The day of the trial, Derrick read a verse from the bible and prayed. After that, he was prepared to face whatever was coming his way.

The prosecutor only had policemen as his witnesses. Derrick had the following facts in his favor, he never went into the bank, he was sitting in the passenger's seat and he did not have a weapon on him. Derrick's attorney made sure to elicit all of those facts from the officers, in front of the jury. He then called Tee to the stand, he was sworn in and seated.

"Could you state your name please?"

"Tavon Williams."

"And do you know the defendant?"

"Yes I do."

"How do you know him?"

"We grew up in the same neighborhood."

"On June 10th you and the defendant were together, am I right?"

"Yeah we were together."

"At some point you pulled into a First Merit bank did you not?"

"Yeah I did."

"You robbed that bank did you not?"

"Yes I did."

"Did the defendant know that you had intentions of robbing that bank?"

"No he did not." When Derrick heard that he let out a sigh of relief, and Stacey smiled. The attorney told the judge that he did not have any more questions. The prosecutor then rose to question Tee.

"Mr. Williams, why would you take somebody with you to rob a bank without their consent?"

"Because I was high."

"Why was the defendant with you?"

"We were at a basketball game together and he stopped me from kicking somebody's ass, excuse me, I mean butt. Then I was supposed to be dropping him off at home, but I made a little detour."

"So you're telling this jury that the defendant had no knowledge that you were going to rob that bank?"

"How many times do you want me to say it? He did not know I was going to rob that bank." Tee then turned to Derrick and said, "I'm sorry for putting you through all that." The prosecutor informed the judge that he did not have any more questions so the judge told Tee to step down.

They had closing arguments, and then the case went to the jury. Within a half an hour the judge was informed that the jury had reached a verdict. Everybody was called back to court, and the judge had the jury's foreman read the verdict, "We the jury find the defendant not guilty of all counts." Stacey put her head down and started crying, and Derrick's parents who were in the back of the courtroom gave each other hugs, Derrick was a free man.

When he got out Stacey told him that she was three months pregnant, and he was ecstatic.

Derrick kept his promise to change his life. He enrolled in college classes at Cuyahoga Community College, and got a job at a steel factory. He and Stacy got married, and his parents put a down payment on a house for them as a wedding gift. Derrick felt bad that Tee was found guilty of murder, robbery and rape and was sentenced to life plus forty years.

36

Spank was released from the county, and went to pick up his car at the impound lot, which had to be returned free of charge. After that, he went to a car wash and had his car washed and waxed, and headed down to Longwood. He wanted to collect his money from Allen and Tink. Spank pulled up to the pool and seen that damn near the whole hood was up there. He was anticipating everyone bum rushing him, but to his surprise no one attempted to approach him, no one even smiled.

He knew that something had to be up. He noticed Tink sitting on the bench, with Coco sitting on his lap. Spank approached him, "Tink what's up?"

"I ain't feeling you no more Spank and you are not welcome down here anymore."

"Fuck you mean? This is my hood."

"The hood ain't feeling you no more, Spank."

"Nigga you still tripping about that shit? You got out didn't you?"

"You ain't freed me, but as of right now we are free of each other."

Spank noticed Allen standing behind Tink, "Al what's up? It's like that?"

"I got love for you Spank, and always will. I just don't agree with some of the things that you stand for, but I wish you the best."

"You think I'm going to let y'all take away from me, what I built?

"Y'all got me fucked up."

"See that's the problem you got yourself fucked up. It ain't never been just you, it was us always. You got beside yourself Spank, it's over." Tink told him.

"Let me get them ins up off of y'all."

"You slow nigga? It's a wrap, you got nothing coming."

"What you think? I'm some type of bitch, Tink. We can work nigga, we can even go to war."

"That's up to you nigga, but you better come correct." Spank thought for a second and realized that he didn't want to fight Tink. If he lost in front of everybody, he could never get his respect back. He told them, "Fuck y'all niggas, I made y'all, I put this hood on the map y'all ain't go be shit without me. Y'all be easy 'til we meet up again." He got in his car and drove off.

He headed out to his house. He figured that he had enough dope and money to put locks on the city by his self. He pulled up to his house and went to the back door. Spank was surprised to see that his door had been kicked in. He rushed upstairs to his bedroom and went to the closet. As he slid the clothes rack back he saw that his safe was gone. His blood started to boil, he was ready to kill somebody anybody. In the box spring he found that the twenty grand he had stashed there was still in place. He wanted to go back to Longwood and confront Tink, but he knew that he had a no win, it would be suicide.

Spank knew in his heart that one day he was going to get back all that he had coming to him. With only twenty thousand left to his name, he decided to go back to Miami. He would chill with Cherry while he plotted his next move.

Tink took over the operation, he was a better leader, and he treated people better than Spank did. Tink knew that it was harder to make money when you had beef. So he met up with Dame to squash it the beef. After the shooting at the courts, the Valley and Longwood entered into a violent time. They often attended the same clubs, and fighting and shooting almost always occurred when they both were in attendance. After Tink and Dame met up to squash the beef, they resumed their basketball competitions. They went as far as doing business together which became very profitable for both of their hoods. Tink opened up many businesses and took a lot of people off the streets and gave them jobs. Tink bought Coco a hair salon which, she named Linda's. He made Allen second in command and his car was upgraded from a Cutlass to a Benz. Allen felt bad for Spank, but after Sean died he was seeing a side of Spank that he did not like, nor agreed with. He knew that in this game, you could only be loyal to those who were loyal to you. Spank was alright, but to him loyalty only flowed one way, his way.

Tink knew that Spank wasn't going to give up that easily. He knew that eventually, he was going to have to meet back up with him. Tink did not want to lay Spank down, but if he had to he would.

Fred started to feel smothered by Shannon, and he missed the excitement of the streets. It wasn't long before they decided to go their separate ways. Fred got deep back into the game. He was even hanging back out with Doc and Ronald, back on the block pumping dope. His insurance company paid off on his claim, and he went a bought a 2009 Super Sport Monte Carlo. Fred felt as if he was back on top of the world. Within six months Fred was back in jail after he served an undercover on three separate occasions. He pled out to two years, and the first person that he called was Shannon, she was right there to listen to all of the lies and the promises that he made. He told her that after he did his bit that he was going to come home, marry her and get a job.

She vowed that she was going to wait on him. Five months later she was pregnant again, by someone else. She told Fred, and he couldn't believe that she played him like that. They stopped communicating, and he ended up doing a rough bit.

Rick regained use of his arms, but remained paralyzed from the waist down. He was fitted with a special wheel chair that was made for young and active people. He never lost his ambition to be a big time dope boy. He was awarded disability, and took all of his checks and invested them into drugs. Rick would ride around the black in his wheelchair selling everything. He sold crack, ecstasy and weed Rick even had a customized van that he rode around selling dope out of. Sometimes no matter what experiences a person might go through they just never change.

So you see, whether it be in LA, New York, or Cleveland it's the same elements in every hood. You got those that keep it gangsta, and those that snitch. You have the ones that stay loyal and the ones that will cut there brother's throat. Some make it to the top of the game, while others spend their whole lives trying to get off the bottom. If you do not agree with me, ask one of the two hundred thousand federal inmates. They will tell you how the feds are in every inner city in the United States initiating numerous conspiracies that are taking down whole hoods. If you think your hood is any different than the rest, then go and put another hood to the test. I bet you that the end results will be one of two things, either death or prison. Which one will you choose?

The End

Spank's Revenge - Chapter 1

Spank and Kris were in Liberty City sitting in Spank's Navigator.

"So when are you going to get back with me?" asked Kris.

"I'm supposed to meet with Hosea tomorrow so I should be hollering at you by the afternoon."

"It's dry and we been losing a hell of a lot of money. The Carol City niggas have been up here serving."

"Don't worry, tomorrow that all comes to an end."

Kris climbed out of the truck, and Spank pulled off. He was on his way home to count the money he had just gotten from Kris. Spank was getting ten keys from Hosea tomorrow.

Spank had come a long way. When he first moved to Miami a year ago, he had twenty grand to his name after being forced out of the game and his hood by his right hand man Tink. He left Cleveland, Ohio and moved down to Miami for two reasons. First, to be with a stripper name Cherry that he met on his first visit, and to plot his revenge on Tink and the hood that turned its back on him.

Spank's goal was to get his money up. He rented a place in Liberty City, and started hanging in the Pork and Beans projects. He sought out to meet people and develop relationships. The first person that he met was Kris, who was half Jamaican. Kris had been in Miami for seven years. He was fresh out of prison, and was looking to come back up in the dope game, but he had no money or a connect. Kris and Spank developed a relationship, and he soon introduced Spank to a couple of hungry cats from Pork and Beans that wanted to come up.

Spank promised them that they would come up together. Cherry's roommate was a Dominican name Angelica, whose boyfriend was deep in the dope game. His name was Hosea, and she introduced him to Spank. Spank told him about his crew and about his vision. Hosea agreed to sell him one key for $14,000 and see where it went from there. Now here it was a year later, and Spank was buying ten keys of dope.

When he got home Cherry was in the kitchen cooking.

"Hey baby, are you hungry?"

"Yeah I can go for something to eat. Just let me go upstairs and handle something right quick." Once Spank came up he bought a house out in South Beach, and Cherry moved in with him. She stopped stripping and focused on school. Spank was paying her tuition. She called upstairs, "Spank I forgot to tell you, Hosea said call him." Spank came back halfway down the stairs. "What did you say?"

"Hosea called and asked me to tell you to call him when you got in."

Spank went back upstairs and called Hosea, "Hello my friend."

"What's the word Hosea? Is everything a go?"

"Tomorrow morning be at the Saw Grass Mall at ten o'clock."

"I will be there." Spank said then hung up. He was happy that they were about to be back on.

Hosea had been out of the states for over a month, and they had run out of work. Niggas from other cities had been trying to move in on them. He was going to make sure that it came to an end. He counted the money and put it in a Gucci bag then went downstairs to eat.

□

Ten o'clock the next day Spank was sitting in the mall's parking lot. He wasn't there no longer than two minutes before a gold Lexus pulled in next to him. Spank grabbed the bag off of the seat and got out of his Navigator. He walked around to the passenger side of the Camry and got in.

"How have you been doing, Poppi?" Hosea asked him.

"I'm doing a lot better, now that you are back. The streets were dry and we were losing money."

"Well your worries are over, Poppi. I have a new pipeline and I will be lowering the prices for you. From now on you will only pay $12,000 a key, is that good?"

"That's great Hosea, thanks my nigga."

"You're a good dude Spank I want to see you prosper. Start doing something with your money, do something legit."

"I hear you Poppi. Let me get out of here before the traffic gets to thick."

"Okay call me when you are ready, my friend."

"Alright," Spank said and climbed up out of the car.

He jumped in his truck and headed home. When he got there he put five of the keys into his floor safe, then he called Kris, "Get everybody together. Y'all meet me at the spot, in one hour."

"We will be there rude boy."

When Spank arrived at the stash house, Kris was there with Nu-Nu, J-Bo, Jamaican Earn and Rocky.

"What's up?" he greeted them when he entered the house.

"You're the man." said Earn.

"I got a brick for each of you. We back on, so don't worry about nothing. We ain't ever running out again."

"I say let's celebrate tonight by going to the King of Diamonds. Then we start going hard tomorrow rude boy." said Kris.

"Y'all go ahead, the wife will kill me. I will get up with y'all tomorrow." Spank told them.

"Okay we will see you tomorrow rude boy."

Spank left the stash house and headed back home. He was going to chill with Cherry. He went home and they had a candlelight dinner, then went up to their bedroom and had wild passionate sex. Afterward, Cherry fell asleep, while Spank laid awake. He could not sleep, his thoughts were on Cleveland. He missed his hometown and his hood. Spank's money was up and he had a team. He was thinking that maybe it was time to go back and get what was taken away from him.

□

The next day he met up with Kris and the rest of the crew. He shot his pitch to them.

"I got some unfinished business back in my hometown. I think now is the time for me to go back and set things straight. I can't do it by myself though, so I want to know if y'all are willing to ride with me." They all felt loyal to Spank. He had kept his promise and put them all on. They felt that his problems were theirs also.

"We are with you rude boy," said Jamaican Earn. That was music to his ears. He got with Hosea, to discuss ways to get his dope shipped to Cleveland. Then he went and explained to Cherry that he had to go back home for a while. She begged him not to go, but Spank told her that it was something that he had to do. He told her that he was going to send for her if he thought he'd be out there for a while.

The following week Spank, Kris and the rest of the crew took off in three separate cars heading towards Cleveland, Ohio. While driving Spank thought to himself, "It's time that we meet up again Tink."

New Flavor Books & Publishing LLC

Book Order form

Full Name: _____

Institution# (If applicable):_____

Address: _____

Address 2: _____

City:_____ State:_____ Zip:_____

Book Title:	Price/Quantity
Hood to Hood: A Cleveland Story	$15.99 ____
Hood to Hood 2: Spank's Revenge	$15.99 ____
Sexual Addiction: Director's Cut	$15.99 ____
All Flavors: A book of Erotic Short Stories	$9.99 ____
Bisexual Bliss	$15.99 ____
Murder or Justice	$15.99 ____
Hittin' Licks	$15.99 ____
Deadly Surgeon	$15.99____

Total Including ($3.00) Shipping and Handling _____

To place an order for one of our books please send a payment
for the price of the book plus $3.00 for shipping and handling to:

New Flavor Books & Publishing LLC

C/O Book orders

P.O. Box 603323

Cleveland, Ohio 44103

Please allow 2 - 4 weeks

www.ingramcontent.com/pod-product-compliance
Lightning Source LLC
Chambersburg PA
CBHW072233170626
46813CB00003B/1203